# JUST KEEP BREATHING

JESSE FRAYNE

Napoleon Publishing/RendezVous Press acknowledges the support of the Canada Council for our publishing program.

Published by Napoleon Publishing/RendezVous Press
Toronto, Ontario, Canada
www.rendezvouspress.com

09 08 07 06 05 5 4 3 2 1

Library and Archives Canada Cataloguing in Publication

Frayne, Jesse, date-
Just keep breathing / Jesse Frayne.

ISBN 1-894917-32-4

I. Title.

PS8611.R39J88 2005 C813'.6 C2005-903471-8

For Mark,
who knows everything I don't

# ONE

Gus dodges Rotation's long-legged kick. He goes to stand outside the racehorse's box stall, hands in his pockets, hat tilted back on his tanned bald head.

"Think about this, Jeanie, I'm telling ya," he says. "Take six to Kentucky next week, I'll start ya off at a grand."

It's after daybreak, the last stakes day of the racing season at Toronto's Woodbine track in southern Ontario. Behind the backstretch, blanketed thoroughbreds sway along the shed rows. Nearby maples are brilliant red, orange and pink, and frost sparkles in the grass. By the middle of next week, all the colour, the gear, the horses and people will have moved on, to the fall 2004 season at Churchill Downs, to the heat in Phoenix, to the rain in Vancouver.

"Y'know, this is a great offer, Jean," Gus points out. "Six horses to train. Okay, two thousand dollars a week, and all the riding you could want." Gus has bright green eyes, that are trying to catch mine on this cold morning. "What's our problem here?"

I gave notice last month; he still acts like it's not happening.

"Jeanie!" He's frustrated. "I don't get it. You're magic with horses. You ask 'em for what they got, and they give it all. I know ya love this business... What's holding you up?"

"C'mon Gus," I plead, turning back to the leathers. "Don't make me feel like I'm letting you down. I'm really sorry...I just can't do this any more."

I'm embarrassed, and so's he. We're silent.

The filly I'm tacking up is one of my favourites, Rotation. She's a two-year-old granddaughter of Neartic and was one of a dozen or so horses that I broke to saddle last year.

"But thanks. You know I'm grateful, Gus, for everything..." He's pacing in the shed row. This happens so rarely between us, we don't know what to do.

Standing beside Rotation, calf-deep in straw, saddle buckles at eye level, I haul the girth up tight. She's been a fine racehorse this season, sure of herself, ambitious, and fast enough to take your breath away. She's swept 'em off their feet at Woodbine for her last five starts, and tomorrow she begins her conquest of the U.S.

"Here you go, Jeanie, let 'er rip." Rotation's groom, a gangly guy in his mid-twenties, nicknamed Tanglefoot for his rangy stride, keeps hold of the bridle and comes around to give me a leg up. I vault up into the saddle. Gus stands back from the stall door, lifting his hand in a placating gesture. We're both sorry, but we're okay.

I pick up the reins and find my stirrups as Rotation steps out of the box stall eagerly, shivering, nosing the air and eyeballing the winking gold leaves outside. As we reach the road, she pops a little, bucking, happy. She's a leggy filly who handles herself delicately, a thousand pounds of shiny red horse pecking along on springy girlish ankles. She jerks the lines to show she wants more headroom.

"Settle down here, goofball," I scold her, letting out more rein. The horse's ears swivel back as she listens. Approaching the gap, Rotation dips her head to stare at the dark underpass that leads to the track. She turns one eye, then the other, pointing her ears at it too, in case it barks.

A cold front of cloud is moving across the perfect sky, turning off the twinkle on the ground. The filly hops sideways, tensing as I bring the shortened crossed reins down on her withers. I lift off the saddle, supporting myself in a balance of hands, knees and feet. We trot through the gap, and there's the track, so wide, so far to the turn. Past us, ploughing down the middle of the raceway, a black mare labours along, her jockey standing straight in the irons over her singing "Don't you run sweet fer me my darlin'". A few other thoroughbreds beat by with their special rhythm, streaming, groaning with effort.

Rotation jumps lightly to see them, bucks twice, then leaps out, reaching hind legs under her, lifting into half-flight, vaulting, throwing herself a bit further each stride. I collect her a little and ride high as she begins her song: her strides, her heart, her lungs and blood and bone, and the earth flying up behind.

Rain starts to fall, washing my face, flattening the filly's fine chestnut hair to her skin. I hold her in, keeping away from the rail. We pass the three-quarter pole well in hand. Rotation has established her pace, fast but strong, as if she could go all day. She's wonderful to ride: smart, neat, always listening.

We glide past the empty grandstand. I work with her, keeping flexible, light-handed, reaching with each of her strides. The white rail flickers by at the left, and on the right I see the gap as we pass, completing the first mile.

As we're nearing the half, I edge the filly over to the inside and let her go. Just click to her, and she flattens herself nearer the ground, reaching her nose out, big haunches stretching. She's like an Austin-Healey sportscar shifting into overdrive. Effortlessly, she finds another way of running, one that doesn't touch the ground or involve the physical limits of muscle or air. Tucked down on her neck, pushing her with hands and feet, it seems to me she keeps finding a crack to slip through, a little time warp crack, silently shoving her big shoulders through space ahead of time. She purrs around the turn, eats up the stretch.

Gus is at the finish, stopwatch snapping in a hand draped over the rail. I lift myself from the crouch and signal Rotation to relax. She slows to a flexy gallop, arching her neck, chin to her broad chest. On the turn there are two horses breezing on the outside, their riders chatting together across their shoulders as they pull their mounts in, slower, slower, ready to turn back and exit through the gap for the walk home. Rotation opens her throat and neighs at them, her body shuddering with the noise, her head up, tail up and whisking, bellowing her challenge to run again. She's in her prime, perfect.

* * *

Back at the barn, Tanglefoot is ready with a bucket to wash the track off the horse. I hold the shank as Rotation fidgets and catches her breath, stamping, her nostrils big as oranges, the veins in her neck and chest beating visibly. Steam curls up her wet red flanks. The groom sings along with the radio: Randy Travis. He sponges the filly's body quickly, scrapes off the water with a curved aluminum stick and settles a gauzy white cooler over her, covering ears to tail and down to her knees. We have nothing to say to each other. Over the years we've gotten along passably well, but we've never been close. I'm not sure if Tangle is close to anyone. He just glances at me as he takes the shank and leads the horse into the shed row path to walk until she's cool.

Gus drives up in his Eldorado. He has snowy hair most of the way around his head, lighting his ruddy, chunky face. He removes the cigar from his heavy lips with the stopwatch hand, pinky finger diamond ring sunk in the soft flesh.

"She run good, Jeanie," he roars from the car, in backstretchese.

"She's in wonderful shape," I chirp. "She go that half in under 45?"

"Better time than she *raced* Tuesday," he thunders. "Dammit, Jeanie, if you don't wanna train, just do some racin' for me, okay? Is *that* too much to ask?"

What? "Aw, Gus, she just likes me 'cause I'm inconspicuous," I call back, confused.

"Hell you are!" His face is red. "In Kentucky, you're real inconspicuous!"

What the hell is his problem? My temper flares up.

"Dammit, Gus, quit shoving, will you? I can't go, that's it. Stop bullying me."

"*Bullying!* I haven't *begun* to bully you, sister. You wait, you'll see bullying." Gus is hot, not his nature at all. But we're in a pissing match now.

"You lay off me, I'm warning you! Cut this out, Gus!"

"Cut *what* out, Mrs. Spring? That I expect fair treatment? Reasonable return? You've got your nerve, little lady."

"What are you *talking* about? Don't give me that crap! I've always been straight with you!"

"Like hell you have! I've a mind to take you to court, you know!"

My jaw drops. Passing as he walks Rotation, Tangle is our witness. He stares at me, with a little bit of a smirk.

Gus and I never fight like this. *No one* fights like this in front of racehorses: it agitates them.

Fifteen years ago, when Gus took me on, he made me the first woman to break his yearlings to track. He taught me what to look for, how to bring it out. It took him a while to trust me, but when he did, his acceptance was unconditional. He's a shy and generous man, not at all a tough guy. He sees Tangle and clamps his teeth around this cigar again.

"Damn it, woman! Your timing here is terrible!"

Off he goes. He guns the engine, push-buttons the window up against the rain and pops gravel all the way around to the shed parking lot. His two training assistants are over there, Joaquin, a wiry Cuban with molten eyes, and an American guy, Meryl, who is leaving this afternoon to do some prep for our season at Churchill Downs. I think they're going to get an earful about how Gus feels toward me at the moment.

His anger still stings. I've never seen him like this. I've hardly even seen *myself* like this. Gus fired up some old memory in me, some sort of dominating devil memory that got my dukes up for a fight.

* * *

I've one horse left today. I'm in the tackroom with Dolly Parton. Music is supposed to relax the horses: these ones sure seem to like country.

I take a breath to calm down. It's ten a.m., a very quiet time at a racetrack. The rain is steady. You can smell linament, and the oats the horses are lunching on, and the peat and straw they have for bedding. Three stalls down, a colt called Pete's Prayer is enjoying a whirlpool, standing with his forelegs knee-deep in a black rubber tank of bubbling epsom salts. His wispy-haired groom, Gabby, sits nearby, keeping the horse company as much as anything, offering him the odd sip of coffee from his cup. Racehorses have no social life with other horses, and, in the way that housepet dogs do, they wire themselves to people. They're individuals. One has a silly sense of humour, another one loves a little kitten, another just hates to wait.

Lots of grooms, exercise boys and hotwalkers live at the track, travelling with their charges from place to place, an insulated social circle laced with trainers and owners, blacksmiths and vets. Jockeys swish through this community like broadway stars, maybe appearing only for the performances. This is a peaceful world, it keeps its own clock, has its own language and humour, maintains its own supports. A private, unbalanced, protected life. On my own, I could do this, I could live like this.

Gabby rises stiffly to his feet, shifts his cap, peering into the rain. One of the track attendants, yellow slicker flapping, is cantering by on his pinto. He waves at us and shouts: "Ned Beatty got tossed into the fence! They're taking him to hospital."

"No! What happened?" We step out onto the road.

"Broke his hip again, they think." He urges the horse and lopes off toward his barn.

"Think that would be the hip with the pin in it, Gabby?"

"Either one, he's going to be off his feed for a while this time." He turns to me. "What the hell's up with you 'n Gus?"

"Got me. Wasn't that awful? I totally blew. I'll have to apologize to him."

"Don't fret about it. You know Gus loves ya, Jeanie. Somethin's troublin' him though, must be."

"Yeah." I slip my arm through his, and we stand quietly. "You want to drop over to Etobicoke General with me later, see how Ned's doing?"

"Naw, I can't, I got Pete's Prayer in the second."

"Oh, yeah. Okay." We come in out of the drizzle and get back to work.

* * *

When I first started at the track, I was just a kid, a hot walker. Gabby'd been a groom for years, and even back then he looked pretty scraggly. Ned was an exercise boy. They and the other steely little men on the shed row suffered me graciously. I was fifteen, weighed a hundred pounds, was socially inept, fierce and horse-crazy. They called me the Little Broad and gave me every break. They fined each other money for swearing in my earshot. Gus trained me, then I trained the horses. I learned to read equine minds, taught yearlings how to look at the ground they were moving over, showed them how to break out of the starting gate, how to hold onto themselves, and how to run. I acquired the trainer's eye and watched enough blacksmiths fitting shoes and vets castrating colts to just about do it all myself.

But I'm done with racing, don't want Gus's offer. May as well ride in the rodeo. Ned's never even gonna walk again, betcha. Where I used to rise into the saddle, focussed on the progress of the horse, now I sit in dread. I've lost it.

* * *

My last ride is Fandangle, who has just been gelded, a few days ago. I'm the lightest rider in Gus's barn, so I get Fandangle, and any other sore ones. I find his bridle and girth in the tackroom, pick up a slicker, and carry my saddle down the shed row to his stall. Fandangle's a big bay horse who's got a bad attitude. Right now, he doesn't know what's hit him. His hormones are humming, he's still real stiff and sore, but he's full of this high octane feed and hasn't been out for some time. He's feeling pretty snakey. He looks at me wall-eyed, jerks around his stall.

I still know how to *do* it. It's just...I'm afraid all the time.

"Okay, big guy, be nice. We'll go smell the flowers." I tie him to the wall ring to saddle him. He fusses and swishes back and forth. I set the stirrups long, like we're going for a walk in the park. His groom doesn't show up, and I have to find someone to help me get up on him. As I lead Fandangle out of his stall, he rushes and bumps himself on the door. This upsets him, and he's too distracted to notice me talking to him. He's spooking at the rain, snorting, tossing his head and planting his forelegs. As we approach Gabby's end of the shed, I call him out of the stall, where he's preparing his horse Pete for the second race.

"Gabby, please, could you give me a hand."

"Sure thing, Jeanie." He dips aside as Fandangle goes for his shoulder with teeth bared. "Colt ain't changed much, eh?"

"Not yet."

Gabby holds the reins in one hand and my shin in the other so I can hike up onto the gelding's twitching back. I reach under my knee and pull the girth snugger. Gabby lets us go, and Fandangle springs down the shed row, out the end, into the rain.

We turn away from the track, to the field that surrounds the barns. There's a path that follows the fence on the outer limit of the track property, where the horses can run gently, no pressure, stretch their muscles and tone themselves on the natural footing. It's soft footing today, getting a bit slippy.

"Steady here, calm down, darling," I soothe, as the horse sashays and swings under me. I try giving him more line, to relax him. I make my body loose, sitting right down. Get the message? We're all fine here. We reach the path, and I let Fandangle ease up to a gallop. I'm ready, watchful, and I'm thinking about a legendary jockey, Avelino Gomez.

"See, Fan-ding-dangle," I croon to the horse. "If I were Avelino, I'd know what to do with a nutcase like you. Gomez was the best." Sighing the words, like a lullaby. Relax, relax.

"When I was a schoolgirl, I was goofy for him," I confide to the horse. "I collected his old press clippings like gumcards. In 1966, he set the record for stakes race wins in a single season, thirty-two. Unsurpassed for thirty-five years, if you want to know. Steady, steady, take it easy now." I firm up my contact a little on the rubber-coated reins. The gelding is galloping slowly, but he's not watching where he's going.

"Avelino knew everything about horses and everything about racing. He'd know about you, you old turd." Singsong. La-la-la.

When I found out that Gus had actually *known* Avelino, I was smitten. I pestered him for stories, asked a hundred questions, wrung Gus for details of the jockey's person and his technique. Amused, Gus indulged me, leaning back in his chair with his mug of coffee, or leaning on the shed row of any barn we'd ever raced from, spinning stories of glory. A few years after his record setting season, on an ordinary day, Gomez was thrown off a very ordinary horse into the same rail Rotation and I were hugging a while ago, and he was killed. Until lately, Avelino's death for me has had the feel of heroism.

Slicker wapping, water dripping off my crash helmet brim, wet hands lying on the slick bay neck. We've been the length of the path, and I pick up the slack in the lines, beginning to rein in. Fandangle tosses off the contact. That's his thing, he hates the rein, it makes him crazy. He begins to run, throwing his legs out, head high, not thinking, racing on rough muddy ground.

"Okay, o-kay, you're fine, easy, ea-sy," I try to talk him down. Fandangle is dishing, bucking, he's hurting himself. "Whoa, now, whoa big guy… You're going to fall down, you big jerk." Fandangle is deep in his own mind, blown on his injury, his isolation, his confinement, his vitamin supplements, the rain, and on me. He's a runaway.

Does luck run out? Where you were safe and careless, now you are at risk and afraid: does this happen? Physically I haven't changed much from those hotwalking days, put on less than ten pounds and no more height at all. And I'm strong, arms and thighs striped with muscle and lungs that don't give up, but of course this is no defence. I sit on this rocket, thinking about it. Thinking I could be home, hugging my kids. I could see Frank once in a while. I don't want to be travelling around from track to track nowadays. This is silly. This sport is dangerous. I don't feel invulnerable anymore. I could get killed.

Fandangle is flying, water shooting up from the field as each hoof strikes the soft muck. He's a really fast racehorse with thousands of dollars worth of insurance on his mighty, and fleeting, value.

"That's enough, now, big guy." I take hold of one rein in both hands and pull Fandangle's head around. He begins to circle, then loses his stride and finally slows, blowing. He's so stiff, he's so dopey, he can't think. He's not meant for this life. I'm looking into his face, he's blinking, trying to make sense. He needs something a lot more low-key. I need something a lot more low-key too. Fandangle comes to a trot, a walk, a standstill.

So, that's it. That's the end of my career. I find there is a limit. Passion is one thing, but you know what? It's not everything. I love racing, but maybe I can't do it any more. Maybe I've lost my nerve.

We walk back to the barn. The horse is spent. I sit on him with long reins and loose feet and see that he finds his way. Fandangle's groom meets us and gives the horse a wash. I feel awful.

I hold Fandangle by the halter and warble horse talk to him until his bath is over. He's confused, pissed off, and hungry, but his legs are fine: he'll live to be a pain in the neck some other day. He goes walking with his groom, striking at him like a huge cobra, trying to kill him. I put my saddle over the shed rail to soap the leather. Rain, radio. Hose off the muddy slicker and hang it up.

I have been mulling for months that this racetrack life is too violent, too far from the beaten track. Today, the pointlessness of Avelino's death has finally changed me. Gus seems strained and vulnerable; something's troubling him, and I hate leaving it on this note with him. But his car is gone. I'll have to call him later. I'm really done.

Rotation is still walking with Tanglefoot, cooling, the sheet peeled back now from her neck. She's a wonder, about the most confident horse I've known, solid in her element.

"Bye, girl," I watch her sway away down the shed row. "Give 'em hell in Louisville."

I wave to Gabby, throw the saddle in the trunk, get in the car and drive home.

# TWO

I get home and stand in the barnyard. The kids are at the sitter, it's very quiet, the rain running through the leaves of the apple trees, and in the barnyard, filling hundreds of hoofprints. Chickens snuggle in the coop, sparrows chirp meekly from the windbreak line of spruce beside the long driveway. Racing has been my life for two decades, its loss feels like panic. I use the phone in the barn to call the production office, to find out where Frank is.

He's on another MOW: Movie Of the Week, also known as a Twenty Day Wonder. For twenty days, you wonder why you're making this movie. Frank wonders how he can make it with only three guys in his department. Wonders about the twitch in his face, the fist in his chest, the iron lock on his neck and shoulders. Maybe he wonders how his family is getting along without him. I get directions and get back in the car.

Each day on this movie, the crew works flat-out for six hours, then breaks an hour for lunch. Then there's the afternoon, six more hours, half hour break for dinner, and then a few hours more. Each day they shoot six or eight pages of script, where an eighth of a page might read something like: "ALIEN SPACESHIP HOVERS, LASERS HIT BANK TOWER, BUILDING EXPLODES, CARS AND SIDEWALK ARE THROWN INTO THE AIR." Okay, so say the spaceship is dangling fifty feet up from an industrial crane, lit by a half dozen 10K's. The special effects guys have flame throwers up there, and there's dynamite in the bank tower, and under the cars, and in the sidewalk, and one take is all you get.

Planning is important. They'll set that scene up and shoot it in a few hours. That's their job, to say yes, and to do it. They keep their jobs by getting it done fast—and without killing anyone.

My windshield wipers set a pace, squeak-thunk, squeak-thunk, and the tires swish through the shallow highway puddles. Some of this movie was shot in studio, around constructed sets; most was on location, like today, which is a sixth day, getting stuff they missed during the scheduled days. A fine day for shooting outside. Those boys will be soaked through.

They're in a field, set up beside a B-52 airplane, which is supposed to have crash landed. As I get closer, I can see that set dressers have arranged mud and grass over the nose and wingtips, and Frank and his crew have rigged twenty-by-twenty frames of sheet plastic as rain cover over the action end of the plane, and over the camera. They've got lights in there to compensate for cloud cover, and plywood on the sloppy, uneven ground to firm the footing.

An Assistant Director, a 3rd A.D., waves me into a parking area out of the way. I put up my umbrella and stand with him to watch quietly.

Frank, and George, his second, have just finished assembling and levelling dolly track. Daniel, the truck grip, runs in with sandbags to brace the last of the supports. "Watch your backs. Coming through." Frank, George and Daniel carry the dolly through the crew and put it on the track. It's a four-hundred-pound hi-tech wagon, but the weight doesn't seem to bother them, and nobody offers to help. Everyone is scrambling with their own tasks, to finish this outdoor stuff before they drown.

The camera assistant sets the Arriflex on the dolly head and clamps it down.

The operator, Dick, who is a pal of Frank's, sits in his place on the dolly, swings the viewfinder to his eye, and they have a rehearsal of the move. George pushes the dolly, starting smoothly and creeping it along the track, thirty feet, in an arc, around the nose of the plane. Frank and Daniel are moving quickly among the lights that the gaffer and his electrics have mounted, setting flags and screens that block and diffuse the output and assure a natural look. George completes his dolly move. Apparently one rehearsal will have to do.

"Final touches, everyone!" Makeup runs in to dab the actor's brow and comb his hair one last time. The boom operator mutters to the sound recordist a joke only he can hear. They both snicker and adjust their headsets.

"Quiet! All quiet, please. Lock it up!" commands the First A.D. Everyone in the field becomes still, they hold what they are doing. There's just the clouds moving, the air.

"Roll sound," says the First.

"Speed," says the sound recordist.

The clapper slates the shot. "Scene 78, take one." Snaps the clapboard in front of the lens.

"Action," the director nods. George nudges the dolly, moves it gradually up to walking pace, guides it round the arc, slows and brakes it. The focus puller rotates the lens, the camera operator finishes his pan and holds on the pilot stepping out of the airplane. They get lucky: a sparrow flies through the frame, over the bomber's dry windshield.

"Cut. Print that. Very nice. Let's do it again." Activity resumes. George pulls the dolly back to the starting position.

I catch Frank's eye, and he waves. The clapper slates take two and the shot repeats. There's relief at the end.

"Cut, check the gate."

"Gate's clean," says the focus puller, peering in behind the lens.

"Okay, that's lunch, ladies and gentlemen," rules the First. "Back in one hour for the unit move to studio."

Frank comes over, smiling, long easy strides. He's a big, lean guy with straight black hair that hangs down his back, and eyes like turquoise. "Hi, Jeanie. This is a nice surprise. You want a beer?" Well, I think a beer would be very nice, considering, and so he leads me to the grip truck, and we climb up into the back out of the rain. George comes in too, so there goes our chance to have a little talk. I put my concerns aside.

Frank opens bottles for his second and for me, and we sit down on apple boxes. "That first take was a nice one, George," he says. They both look about tired enough to croak. George is a mountain-sized person, over six feet, maybe 220 pounds. He's wearing a fleece vest under a muddy Gore-tex shell, and his forehead is covered by a yellow bandanna tying back his bushy hair.

"Yeah, we got it, didn't we, buddy. The bird was perfect."

"Gotta hand it to this guy—he's lucky," Frank winks at me. "Director couldn't pay money and get that bird."

"Just as well." George drains his beer and opens another. "So, Jeanie, you guys goin' anywhere after this?"

"Be enough for me if we go have a nice nap, George," I say. "Been a long season. You?"

"Janey and me are going to do the Mexico thing," he says, with humour. "We might carry on a bit and see some of Costa Rica, may as well, once we get down there. Janey's going to take some time, she's near the end of her contract."

George and Janey don't have kids. She's the art director on a long-running TV series. They both work hard and save money then disappear for a couple of months together. We pay our back taxes and the Zellers bill then go to Pizza Hut. Frank must miss goofing off like George can, especially after a nut-wringer like this movie.

"Yeah, Mexico, that's cool," Frank says. "Jeanie and I'll figure out something too." He shifts his position, easing his back against a stack of scaffolding. "Anything. I swear, I catch myself doin' another one of these damn things, I'm gonna open my veins."

George agrees. "No planning! No gear! Hours of set-up for scenes we don't shoot. Director has no idea what he wants..."

Frank takes off his cap and rubs his forehead. "Not even. I mean, bustin' ass to make a movie I don't want my kids to see. I've had it with this garbage."

"Hey, man. Four of these worthless pieces of crap in a row, but we're loggin' close to a hundred paid hours a week. Called payin' the mortgage, Frankie."

"Yup. And after a while, that's not enough. How long do you pay these dues, anyway."

George looks at me, but I have nothing to add. He fires a look at his boss. "Steady, man, you sayin' you're quitting? You're good at this, you know, Frank. I wouldn't jump up and do anything rash."

"Not what I'm saying, George. I like gripping, it's good for me. I like to solve the problems, every one of them different. I like the technical invention part. But I want, you know, quality—work that will mean something to someone, express something for them, make life richer. I want to go home at night feeling like I've contributed something. Same as everybody, I guess. Not this dopey stuff about aliens force-landing a B-52 and then eating it."

"Yeah, Frank, right on man." He finishes his beer. "Wow, I gotta eat."

"I'll come with you. You eat yet, Jeanie?"

"No, I'll come." We hop down off the truck and boot through the flat, frost-bitten grass to lunch.

George continues. "Like with your motorcycles, Frank. I remember years ago you'd tune those old mothers, tinkering, sending away for parts, sweating over 'em until they ran and looked *perfect*. You gotta lower your standards, man."

Frank laughs. "That's it, George! That's where I slipped up. Got a problem? Just gotta lower your expectations!"

"Glad to help out, Frank." We are approaching the lunch tent. It looks dim and dry in there. "Why'd you quit with those motorbikes, anyway?"

"Oh, you know, George." Frank lets me go in the tent before him. "Sooner or later, everyone has a car accident. On a bike, it's just so much worse."

* * *

The eighty-odd cast and crew members are seated at long fold-out tables arranged all over the inside of the tent. Steam trays are lined up on tables across one side, cafeteria style, where two young women are still serving dry sliced turkey and limp grey vegetables.

"Holy smoke," Frank says to me. He turns around to

go back outside. "Jeanie, there's nothing to eat here! Oh...the salad looks okay."

"And it's a long day, fella. What's up with George?"

"You know him. He can only make sense when it matters." Frank takes some bread and salad and a few slices of turkey and makes a sandwich. George is ahead of us, and he likes brown and white food. His plate is piled. I don't really feel like eating. We all sit down with the electrics. Dick, the operator, is there too.

"Jeanie! What, you still married to this guy?" He elbows Frank's ribs. "How're the ponies?" Dick's about fifty, with lots of curly silver hair everywhere and a good many belts and buckles on his outfit. He's a very jovial guy with an excellent professional reputation, but I haven't found much to like about him personally.

"Just wrapped up this morning, Dick. You getting your day?"

"We're getting the shots, yeah, but it's absolutely nuts, one thing after another, eh, Franklin?"

"Well, yeah," Frank bites into his sandwich. "Start things off, when I get here there's a message from Daniel that the truck won't start. So there's all our stuff, everything we need to start work, stalled in the studio parking lot. Daniel says he's getting a jump and should be along, that's how he puts it. 'I should be along.'"

Dick interjects. "And here's the sun coming up for this dawn shot they want, and the producer is pacing back and forth and smacking his forehead, like it's the end of the world..."

"The guy's close to tears," Frank takes back the floor. "Meanwhile, the director and the director of photography are discussing how they want the first shot to look. He wants the dolly move that you just saw now…" waving out toward the plane, "…here to here. So they start: makeup and wardrobe and cast are still in the honeywagons; electrics are humping cable and lightstands over the frost—there was *frost* in the grass this morning…"

"Really cold this morning," comments George, shovelling in his grey carrots.

"…and the camera department and director are milling, waiting, checking their watches, Jean…and the sun is starting to come up."

"So here, bucking into the pasture, headlights swinging, Daniel at last, and we tear open the doors and just *throw* equipment out of the truck, laying track like maniacs, when we get the voice on the radio, not doing that shot now, don't need that now. He wants to do a crane shot up, looking into the cockpit to see the survivors. Okay, all the better, we get the crane out…"

"About then it starts to rain, Franklin."

Frank nods. "We do another crane from the other side to see the bloodstreaked pilot, and it starts to rain. It's not heavy, we think we can finish.

"The survivors recover consciousness and get out of the plane, overcome! Thrilled to be alive! Take after take. There's a guy with one line he can't remember. We must have done that scene, what, twenty times, George? Rain is pouring down by now, Daniel's put the plastic up, we could have been in the studio for the whole thing. There's this fantastic reconstruction of the airplane built in the studio…"

Valeria comes in the tent. She's the locations manager that everyone has a crush on. She's tall and blonde and dreamy and hugs everyone regularly. George straightens his shoulders as Valeria sits down with him.

Dick picks up the story. "Now they want to set up from the southeast side of the plane to see the people emerge, the reverse angle, but when cover is moved and the camera is in position and the lights are aimed and it's all ready, he realizes this isn't what he wants, and it's not going to match the rest of the footage we shot last week. So everything is moved to the west side of the plane, right? And was there rain? Why, yes, there was. Rain does not match either."

"We have a B-52 in the studio..."

"Going to the wrap tonight, Dick?" Valeria is eating a piece of chocolate cake.

Dick gazes at her for some time but refrains from removing his clothes. "I guess so, I'll see how I'm feeling, um, later. You up for it?"

"I wouldn't miss a party." She closes her eyes and tips her head back. "I need some dancing."

There's perfect silence at the table. In a moment, George resumes chewing. The electrics clear their throats and stand up.

"Valeria, this is my wife, Jeanie," Frank stands up. I shake her hand. "I need to go back to the truck, Jean, are you pretty set?"

"Sure thing." How will George and Valeria find a place today, I wonder, with all this rain? They are leaning together as we head out of the tent.

"So, how're you doing, Jeanie? Been so wacky here, our last day of shooting..." He's looking at me for a clue, but I haven't got one.

"Finished up at the track, honey. I'm a loose goose."

"Great! Must feel good." He's not listening. But also, I'm not telling. Since I gave Gus my resignation, I've not mentioned the track to Frank. There's always so much other stuff to squeeze into the ten minutes a day we have alone together. It seems like a long time since we saw each other eye to eye.

He keeps walking quickly to the grip truck. "Geez, I hate this season. The rain, this flat grass, the shadows under the trees. The end of mercy. It's creepy. I need…oops," he snorts to himself. "I mean *we*, Jeanie, *we* need a vacation."

"Good thought, Frank." I'm speaking to his back. He climbs into the truck. Daniel is there, and when I come in, his boots are thick with mud, rain still dripping from his cap brim. He's been wrapping stuff into the truck by himself.

"Hi, Jeanie. Frank, this is a big fuckin' mess, here, man. There's muck splashed up into the wheel *bearings*, even. We gonna have to have all this stuff overhauled."

"Got what we need for the rest of the day, you think?"

"Shit, maybe, I dunno. What's left to do?"

Frank pulls his callsheet out of his pants pocket and studies it. "Not too much, the studio cockpit of the crash itself, with the gyro platform. I'll call the equipment house and see about another dolly."

"I guess I'll be off, honey," I say, edging toward my car. "Gotta…"

"Okay, that's okay, thanks for dropping by, Jean. We should be done about… Oh, wait!" He's just remembered. "The wrap party is tonight. Wanna go?"

"Sure, well, I'll have to see about getting a sitter…"

"My cell is in the pickup," he says, stepping down off the truck. "Okay? I'll walk you."

He's beat. Through my rainy windshield, I watch him punching his phone, in his maxi-cab with the heater going. He's resting a minute, putting in his equipment order, sorting out his afternoon. I know what he said to George is the truth: not the money, the meaning. We've got to get some time together, this is ridiculous.

# THREE

My last day at the track, Frank's last day on the airplane movie. We've reconvened at the wrap party.

The kids were very happy that I invited them. After I checked on Ned at the hospital, I picked up the kids from the sitter, took them out for pizza, then met Frank here. Holding Lukie on my hip, I pick another carrot stick for him from the buffet table and look around for my husband in the crowd. He is in the swirl of mud-caked technicians, gesturing with his beer to someone, describing something. Our two six-year-olds have found him. Indianna and Zazie droop at his sides, each hanging on a pantleg. Most of the film crew members have brought their families tonight. The kids have been chasing one another in the forest of adult legs until they're ready to drop.

Frank's peers are mainly in their late forties. They once rallied for peace and women's lib, attended V.D. clinics and Odetta concerts, tripped with acid and religion, and then backpacked through Europe. So many of the same Baby Boomer mold, and all ancient history now. The idealism of their twenties has now firmly settled. Crafts they liked and developed became careers in which they are now leaders. Now it's okay to make money. In fact, who can remember when it was embarrassing to make money? They buy new, never-before-used clothes, designer furniture. They have monogamous relationships and they buy and sell houses. Some of them have done all that twice: those are the ones here with the babies. The rest have teenaged kids. Frank is a member of both groups.

Ten years younger than my guy, and born poorer and rural, I missed this boat, or went on a different one. I was never hip: I was always in the barn.

These guys, these younger technicians arriving now, with two-tone hair and no mortgages, are from some other planet far from mine. I see them revving up for the dancing and notice that they don't see me. I don't count, I'm invisible.

Frank's first wife is now a film producer in Los Angeles. Their teenage daughters fly up three or four times a year and stay with us a week or two each time. I think the farm bores them, but they're lovely kids, they care about their dad, and they've let me get close to them.

It's a nice party. Great room. It was once a dance school, has that high ceiling, fourteen-foot windows, and the tongue and groove flooring worn smooth as leather. Dancers begin to warm up as the band slides into a conga reggae. The band is barefoot, drinking mineral water. Every one of them can play eighty-five instruments and simultaneously sing harmony. The music is complex, fluent, really big, and it's making me feel happy.

Valeria, the locations manager, is dancing with Dick-head the camera man. She fulfills all of my preconceptions about her dancing. Further, I feel they deserve each other. And there's George, Frank's dolly grip, and his pal Janey, sailing around like there's no yesterday. Tomorrow they go on vacation, lucky them.

"How's that, Lukie?" I snuggle my words into his neck. "Loud, eh?"

"I yike it, Mom!" Our boy is three, and hasn't been to a dance since he was a nursing infant. His little face is glowing with the excitement of the party, happy. A dear person is in there.

A few people are shooting pool at the tables in a corner of the room, under nice low green-shaded lights. The star of the movie is there. She has a huge reputation of her own, but it's her husband who is the really famous one, name-dropped, talk-showed, awarded. They're playing pool together, with a discreet crowd of onlookers. Everyone is very cool about it, about his celebrity status, no autographs or fuss at all, just pool. I can't keep myself from peering over that way every couple of minutes, watching him bend over, into the yellow light, or stand hipshot, chalking his cue. Frank is on the dance floor, waltzing with his daughters. He signals me as they zoom by. The room is a cloud of heat and colour and noise.

We can hear each other better in the hallway. "These girls have had it," he reports, as the two of them disappear into the washroom. "I wish we'd gotten a sitter, Jean, the party's just getting going and we have to leave." One of his pals passes, and Frank greets him, turning away from me.

"Hey Tom! How you doing?" Tom makes a response I don't hear.

"Yeah, we're just leaving," Frank groans. "Kids!" He gives the "what can you do" shrug. Tom peers around at me, the offensively reproductive parent, smiles, and leaves. Frank turns back.

Lukie is standing with us, twisting on my hand. "Well, it was great for them to come," I say. "They've had a wonderful time. Need some notice to get a sitter, Frank."

He's bigger than life. "Ha ha, that's show biz, eh! No one knows anything until it happens. Hi, girls," he greets our squirts as they come out of the ladies' room. "We'd better find our coats."

"I'm not tired, Dad! I don't want to go," says Zazie, hopping, watching the dancefloor.

"I'd like to stay too, baby, but it's pretty late for Lukie, almost nine thirty," he consoles.

"Stay, Frank, it's okay, I'll take them home." I don't care.

"What, and hang around here by myself? No, I'll come now. I have to get up early for the survey tomorrow anyway, and Dick wants to try out my rig for a shot they're doing Tuesday on that rock video."

"A survey? I thought you had Sunday off." He doesn't answer.

"Can I have more juice, Mom?" says Zazie, clutching her throat.

"We're just going, duck, you can get some at home." I'm wrestling with the bulging coat rack. Lukie, dressed, is tugging me toward the door.

"Hey, Dick!" Frank clasps the cameraman's hand as he passes.

"Yo, Franklin Spring!" He thuds Frank on the shoulder, glances up. "You made it, eh, Jean?"

"Hi, Dick." The "head" is silent. "What's this about a survey tomorrow?"

His face crinkles up in a big smile that leaves his little blue eyes blank. "We're out there, yes, ma'am. Pickering! Or someplace… Franklin, what about that crane shot?

It's gotta go from the driver's lap, up through the sunroof and then out over the gravel pit..."

"Oh, yeah, it'll be okay, I can rig an extension that will cover it..." I've been dismissed from the conversation and stop listening, bending to help Indy with her coat. Indy's face is hot on my cheek.

"I had a good time at Dad's party, Momma," she says quietly.

"Me too, sweetie. Let's say goodbye to everyone now and get going." I'm irritated with Frank, that he's endlessly focussed on his work. Well, it's disappointment, since I thought we were going to have some time together, and now he's working. Hold on... it's anger, dammit, what is this? Last minute invitations? Unannounced changes in schedule? He gets so carried away, so self-involved, he forgets us. How can he goof off like this? Why did he invite me, anyway?

I finish helping the girls dress as Frank shares some parting jokes with his workmate. Phooey on him.

"Well, Franklin Spring, have a fine evening," says Dick. "Jean, divorce this guy, for God's sake." He laughs and throws an arm around my shoulders. I make my face grin and herd the kids outside.

* * *

The sky has cleared, there are stars everywhere, the parking lot is bedded with soggy oak leaves.

"Is there a problem, Jean?" He's a bit drunk. I think he's wondering about that crack of Dick's.

"Skip it, Frank. Here, let me drive." I buckle Luke into his car seat. I don't want to be drawn out now. I don't feel that generous.

Dismissing Frank makes him angry. He helps Indy with her seatbelt and then gets in behind the steering wheel. "You get a lot out of the snotty bitch thing, Jean?"

Leaning over Zazie, looking at Frank over the seat. I don't want to get in the car with him.

"Sorry. Come on," he says, reading me. "I didn't mean that."

I get in and we drive home, discouraged. The girls hum to themselves in the back seat, yawning. Luke, like a tulip, tips over in sleep.

* * *

The answering machine is blinking as we come in. Frank carries Luke to his bed and then goes into his office to return his calls. Zazie and Indianna come with me upstairs and haul off their party dresses.

"I liked that guitar guy, Mom, he was cute," Indy says. "Ooo, can you fix my jammies? There's a knot." She's quite flushed. Maybe it's passion, maybe it's embarrassment at wanting help with her nightie. She's a serious, solid kid, patient with tedious tasks, very meticulous, spends a lot of time in her head. Lucky at cards, a math whiz, great ear at the piano, a precocious painter, and a planner, a problem solver.

"I liked the balloons!" says Zazie, brushing her teeth heartily, oblivious to the little flecks hitting the bathroom mirror. Zazie never asks for help with anything. She thinks she knows the best way to do everything. She doesn't conceal her light beneath any bushels whatsoever. A fireball, like a force of nature: ferocious, explosive, willful. No help at all with farm chores, but she likes to light up the barbecue with Dad and char things.

She finishes brushing and hops up into her dim top bunk. Indy snuggles below. I sit on the chair beside them to sing their sleeping song.

I feel weary from a day of self-evaluation. I've dropped my racing career, and I don't think there was a choice in that, but I want to blame Frank. I know that's outrageous, that it's just so I won't think about how I feel. *Two working parents means the kids are raised by surrogates.* My anger draws me away from him. I stew over my resentment, finding things to hate about him. There's a pain in my chest. I know I'm doing this to myself.

I hear his office door open downstairs. He's off the phone. There's the tread of his boots up the stairs, and his big shape backlit in the bedroom doorway.

"Hello, my little dears," softly, so gentle. When he leans across me to kiss his girls goodnight, I scoot out of the way and go to undress Luke. He sees me dart out the door. I catch his eye, I know he thinks I'm being prickly and unloving. He's right, I am being prickly and unloving. In with his daughters, Frank's deep voice is a tender rumble and the words indistinct.

Lukie is still in his overcoat, the steamy hairs around his ears stuck to his head. He stirs and wakes as I peel off his clothes, arrange his overnight diaper, zip up his sleepers. He's peaceful, gazing out the window at the sparkle in the sky.

"Do aw stars have soyar sisters, mom?" Ah-hah, he's been talking to his father.

"There's planets around every star, little duck. Every star is a sun, like our sun, shining." The floor squeaks behind me as Frank leaves the girls' room and walks the length of the hall to our bedroom. Luke burrows under his covers, I kiss his cheek. "Goodnight, Mr. Boy, see you when you wake up."

"Goodnight, Mrs. Mom." Without moving, he kisses his pillow, smack.

I go downstairs to open myself a beer. I want to sort out my feelings.

I love the kids. I'm glad to give up racing dangerously, in order to focus more on them. It feels weird, but I know it's right. Also, I miss Frank. We've been working apart for months. We don't see each other much, when we see each other, we don't talk, and when we do talk, we argue.

I look after the family and work the horses and our farm, and he does his work and brings home most of our money. When he spends time with the kids, he's very attentive, and they adore him. But he's not here much.

I feel I'm raising these kids by myself. He drops in, charms us all, changes his clothes, and disappears. Our lives are unconnected, and this bad stretch has gone on a long time.

So, change it, Jeanie. Support him. He's working his ass off! You think he likes never having a day off? See it from his side. Be more flexible. Apologize and quit whining.

I mull and putter. The dog, Marilyn, goes out and comes back in. I look at the moon awhile. I have another beer.

The phone rings, mighty late for farmers.

"Jeanie? Gabby here. Got some awful news..."

"Oh, Gabby, is it Ned...his hip?"

"Well, it's another story entirely, Jean: Gus has been hurt."

"Good Christ! Is he okay?"

"Nope."

"What in the world...?" I'm stunned speechless.

"Police found his car on the track parking lot, him dead in it, lotta blood."

"I'll be right there."

"Don't, Jeanie. They're mostly finished now. Just you had to know. The guys are saying yuh should come in tomorrow and straighten things up here, like, with all the horses. Least till we figure this out with the owners..."

"Okay... But, what about Meryl and Joaquin? They're the assistants."

"Yeah, well, Meryl's in Louisville already, and Joaquin's been detained."

"What, you mean, held for questioning? He'd never hurt Gus."

"They were seen arguing in the parking lot."

"Oh, man, what a mess. Okay, I'll see you there at six, no wait, it'll have to be seven thirty, I gotta bring the kids."

"Okay, Jeanie."

His voice stays in my ear. I hang up and hang on to the edge of the table. The world has just tipped up, and everything has slid off.

I turn out the lights and climb the stairs. Frank's asleep, his long, strong exhausted body restoring itself, charging up for tomorrow's challenges. Let him lie. I get under the duvet and have a good look at the ceiling.

# FOUR

The moon passes across the sky, and eventually the radio alarm clicks on at the end of a pop song, and Frank sits up. Clock says 5:44 a.m. Still dark, and the room is chilly, but there are some peeps from the chickadees outside. Frank gets up and turns on the little yellow light on his side. I'm grateful the night is finally over.

"Sweetie, Gabby called after you went to bed. Gus has been murdered."

He's picking his clothes for the day, sleepy, and he can't believe what he just heard.

"Murdered?"

"I don't know anything about it. I'm going to the track this morning to see if the horses can get shipped. Gabby said that Joaquin is being questioned."

"Christ, Jeanie. Why didn't you wake me up?" He sits on the bed near me. "How can I help you? I could come with you? Or stay with the kids while you go?"

"I've been thinking about it, and I'm going to take them over with me. They're comfortable on the shed row, and I can tuck them away from whatever investigation is going on. Gabby will watch them."

Frank is looking at me closely.

"I won't be long anyway," I say. "I'll just hang around a while, do the paperwork. Go ahead with your survey, Frank, and I'll call you if it gets wacky."

He puffs his cheeks. "Just let you handle everything."

Frank straightens, rakes the hair up off his forehead, to fall down his bare back. This is an old battle.

"No really, it should be a couple hours, tops."

"This is one of those times, Jeanie, where I could be more helpful to you. You could let me help you, sometimes."

"I appreciate that and thanks, Frank. I don't see fighting about this. I'm okay with my plan as it is."

"Fine." It's not in the least fine, but he agrees not to fight about it. There are lots of times, lately, where Frank quietly agrees not to fight with me. I see him flit a glance at me now, baffled, suppressed, unresolved. I don't know what to do with it. I'm an adult, I should know what to do with our struggle, and I don't.

We stand up, and Frank takes his clothes to the bathroom where he will shower and shave. I look out the window. Not daybreak yet and we're arguing. I know I'm stubborn, but I want to have some kind of control over this thing. It's so crazy, and it scares me, and I want to be the one to decide how it will play out. How some of it will play out, anyway. And I want the kids near me. They're my shield.

I dress and go into the bathroom when Frank comes out. In the adjacent room, Luke has his tape machine going, Robert Munsch. I scrub my teeth and look at myself in the mirror, the hazel eyes, short shocks of brown hair, small features and freckled skin. I stick my head in the girls' bedroom. Indy's sitting on the thick carpet, holding a stuffed zebra, her fine dark hair a soft cloud around her face.

"You feeling okay this morning, Indy?"

"I have a little headache." Her forehead is warm.

"Yup, I think you're workin' on something here,

tootsie. But I have to go to the track for a while this morning. Are you well enough to come along?"

"Sure, Momma."

"Me too!" says Zazie, heels hitting the floor. "I'm coming to the *track!*"

"Okay, guys. I'm going to start breakfast. How you doin', Mr. Yukie?" He's shuffling out his door.

"Wait, Mom! I want to make my breakfast!" Zazie pushes past me out of her room. "I'm going to make *toast!*"

I follow Zazie downstairs. Luke trails behind us. "Mom, I tey you my dream. There was this dragon, and he roared! RRRRHHHH! Very yowd! And I said, 'Get outta here, you big dragon.' He was very scary."

"Wow, Luke, a dragon with fire and everything?" We've reached the kitchen. Frank is putting on his coat. Zazie pours her juice and plops a slice of raisin bread into the toaster oven. She likes to see the elements come on inside.

"Yes, and a green back, yike a snakey." Luke climbs onto a chair and turns on the little TV. *Toad Patrol* flips and steadies on the screen.

"You're very brave, big guy," I tell him. Indy drifts in and sits down quietly at the kitchen table.

Frank gulps the last of his coffee. "Okay, kids, I hope you have a great day. I gotta go to work," he says.

"We're going to the track, Dad," says Zazie.

"Yeah, Zaz, your mom told me." He hugs her, puts a kiss on Luke's head, ruffles Indy's hair, goes out the door. "Bye, Jeanie. Hope it's not too weird over there."

"Thanks, Frank." I pour Cheerios into a bowl for Luke, who takes his spoon in his fist.

Out the big kitchen windows, I can see Frank walking toward the barn and the shed where his pickup is parked. Marilyn is frisking around, barking at starlings. The sky is pink. So much for apologizing and trying harder. If I were going to fix this, I blew it; though Frank, unaware of my line of thinking, seems okay with my lack of success. We carry on, without resolution, as usual.

I reach the peanut butter down from the shelf and trade with Zazie for the pitcher of juice. "Anybody want an egg? We gotta eat up and get going, kids."

* * *

Full sunlight by the time we get to the track. The shed row where Gus's horses are stabled is disorderly, with straw and hay bales strewn around, coolers thrown on the ground, cargo boxes open and half-packed. Body brushes, shanks, blankets and whirlpool tanks are jumbled on the grass. The upper half of each stall's dutch door is open, and horses are gazing out, but the crashcaps and transport leggings that they should be wearing are still in baskets all down the shed row. Gabby's in the tackroom packing saddles and sees us coming. My stomach is flippy, and I try to brace myself for what will happen this morning.

"Police are here, Jean. They want to see yuh about Gus." Poor Gabby is teary, and he's got whiskey breath. He's had a rough night.

I hug him. "Okay, sweetie. Where's Tanglefoot?"

"Feed room."

"Take the kids to him, can you? We'll talk in a bit."

"Yes, ma'am." He sniffs and turns his attention to them. "How you guys doing, anyway? Ain't seen yuh fer weeks..."

On the other side of the shed row, the parking lot is

full of policemen and squad cars. Gus's Cadillac is still parked there, ringed with yellow plastic police tape and surrounded by little flags stuck in the wet ground indicating footprints. Gus himself is not on hand, though his blood is all over the driver's seat. I turn away quickly and head for the office, where there are some people standing in the open door. Two of them are grooms, Irene and Phil, and there's a guy I recognize as a trucker, who would be here to transport the thoroughbreds. Obviously, everybody's upset over the violence done to Gus, and the absence of his assistant Joaquin makes for more confusion. Tensely, everyone is bending over the paperwork, and when I come in they stand back from the desk and greet me with relief.

"Okay! Jeanie, good," says Phil, pulling me over by the arm. "Jesus, this is the worst day of my life." He's a little guy with curly hair sticking out from under a baseball cap, wearing a jean jacket and work boots. His lean face is crowded around his tight mouth.

"I know! Man, this is terrible for everybody." I hug him for a second.

"Somebody completely crazy did this, that's for sure. Poor Gus. And who knows what's going to happen now, what we're supposed to do here?"

"I've spoken with the people in Louisville, and we're to postpone shipping... What have you got here, Phil?"

"Yeah, here's the thing, look at this, this is pretty screwed up here..." Sliding shipping documentation out of the file folders open in front of him on the desk. "We got these fourteen to go to Kentucky. That flight is, like, in three hours, and they ain't even bandaged yet. And this cop wants t' talk to you, that guy over there, see him? And I can't find the sheets, and I'm not half packed..."

"That's okay, Phil, hold everything," I say. "We're gonna postpone shipping for today, there's just too much to deal with, eh? When I talked with Meryl down at Churchill Downs, he suggested it, and he's rescheduled the flights and informed everybody. Okay? So just take it slower, we have an extra day to get this together. Everybody ships out tomorrow afternoon."

Phil does relax a bit. "All right, Jean. So I can just leave this to you, eh?" Indicating the trucker who's still standing there, a fella I've seen every season for years.

"Yup, we're good here," I nod, and Phil and Irene leave to resume packing. "So, Ricardo," I say to the trucker. "You maybe didn't hear all about this? You'll be loading over at Stafford Farms' barn today, we've done a switch-around with their flights." Stafford is just two sheds over. "Then tomorrow we need you hot and ready at one p.m. Everybody goes at once, two trucks, two flights, no waiting."

"Hey, I just want my cargo, I'm fine with this if you are."

I go for the files. It takes just a few minutes to get Ricardo squared away with his revised transport orders on our horses. He goes out, past the crowded parking lot to his semi, climbs up into the cab and fires up the engine.

Alone in the office now. As I start going over the checklists for the move, a stranger approaches the door. He is large and thick, wearing a blue raincoat and, peculiar in a barn, glossy soft shoes.

"You are Mrs. Jeanie Spring?" He has a loud voice.

I nod at him.

"I am Lieutenant Detective Brock, with Toronto Homicide." Holds up his badge. "I wonder if I might ask you a few questions about the death of Mr. Augustus Hampton."

"Sure." Earlier, when Gabby said "police", I could have pictured Lt. Det. Brock. Here's a guy who knew from childhood he'd be a cop. Got the crewcut, the heavy stubble on the lantern jaw, the sharp blue eyes. No nonsense, mister.

"You were at work yesterday," he says.

"I was here until about eleven o'clock in the morning."

"Where was Mr. Hampton when you last saw him?"

"Gus was…in his car. He drove over from the grandstand. We talked, on the other side of the shed row there, about the horse I had just worked. Then he drove over here, I believe, to the office."

"You have been in his employ how long?" he says.

"Do you have many questions, sir? Because we're really behind here…"

"This is just a preliminary. How long did you work for the deceased?"

"Sixteen years."

"Can you tell me who you think might have killed him?"

"Gus was a very decent person. He was fair to his employees, and he had our respect. He was a gifted racehorse trainer, who worked hard for his owners. He sent his ex-wife a substantial alimony, and he quit drinking ten years ago. I have no idea why this happened to him. I would really appreciate if we could continue this later, this afternoon, or tomorrow morning would be fine."

"Did you know that the Assistant Trainer, Joaquin Alvierez, and Mr. Hampton were lovers?"

I reflect for a minute on how my agenda has not been heard. Next I think about this hard-nosed detective, and how far his non-prejudicial training will bring him. And why does he think this is pertinent, anyway?

"Years ago, when they were lovers, they were good for each other, very close," I say. "Joaquin helped Gus dry out. Their work together has continued to be a bond. Joaquin is not a killer."

"Do you know the subject of their argument last night?"

"No." Outside the office, the cargo bins are being packed. Irene is folding blankets plucked up from the gravel driveway. Phil is moving from one stall to the next one, serving feed: non-flyers can eat. Tanglefoot, Gabby, and my children are out of sight on the other side of the shed row.

"You gave in your resignation to Mr. Hampton last month?"

"Yes," I say.

"Was your termination amicable?" The phone is ringing. I am beginning to feel really pressured by this guy.

"I thought it was."

Ring!

"I still have five of Gus's 'breds on my farm, our working relationship wasn't over. I wanted to leave racing for personal reasons."

"What reasons."

Ring!

"Detective, please...."

"You were seen arguing with Mr. Hampton. Quite a loud argument. Three people heard you shouting at each other. But you say your relations were amicable."

"Good God, what are you asking me?"

RING!

I grab the receiver and bark into it. "Hello! ...yes... yes, we'll need both of those... Right, Marchmount is coming in from the farm. Be here by noon, okay? Okay." Bang the receiver back down.

"I am asking you where you were at the time Mr. Hampton was killed." Brock is looking at me steadily. I can barely move my lips.

"At a party. A hundred people saw me there."

"Thank you for your cooperation, Mrs. Spring. I won't keep you any longer."

* * *

I'm holding myself together, quite well, really. What good will it do anyone to have me freaking out here? Tanglefoot is showing Lukie how he measures feed for the horses. One canister of oats, a half of flax seed, one of vitamin supplement pellets— they both pause to have a sample of these delicious horsey treats—and one of mixed wheat germ, soya and barley mash stirred with molasses. This all gets dumped into galvanized feed pails, and Luke mixes it vigorously with a paint stick. Tangle checks the chart for the supplements each horse receives. EquiBiotic for this one, acidophilus for that one. These horses are athletes, after all: you are what you eat. Luke staggers down the shed row to help Tangle deliver the pails. Thank God for routine tasks.

Tangle glances up at me, over Lukie's head, an odd look, but I'm distracted and don't try to figure it out.

Zazie and Indy have been in a vacant stall, playing with a litter of kittens.

"Would everyone be okay to leave in about fifteen minutes?" I call out, generally.

"I'm ready to go, Mom." Indy looks mighty uncomfortable. I think her cold is catching up with her.

"Okay guys, ten or fifteen, off we go." My voice sounds pretty normal. I scoot back around the breezeway, looking for Gabby. He's in with Pete's Prayer.

"Are you okay, dear?" Touch his shoulder.

"Oh, Jeanie, this is terrible." Pete is standing free, in a blue-checkered sheet. Gabby's kneeling in the straw, rubbing witchhazel into the knees and tendons of Pete's forelegs, and clearly not feeling okay. White whiskers, deeply creased cheeks, the wispy dishevelled hair, rheumy eyes watering, his slacks on a bit sideways, a hole in his sweater.

I squat down beside him. "So...tell me what happened."

"Well, like I told you on the phone, the track police found Gus in his car, lotta blood all over..."

"Where was the car?"

"Out there, same as now, in the parking lot."

"And about what time was this?"

"Half past eleven, I guess, I was in my room sleeping, when the hubbub woke me, the Toronto police arriving. I came out and they asked me if I'd seen or heard anything."

"Had you?"

"Naw. 'Course, Pete's right beside the parking lot here, he's awake and naturally he's spooked 'cause of all the people and lights flashing and whatnot. Bumped up his knees a little bit, I think, swishing around..." Gabby indicates the puffiness on the horse's legs.

"So...you didn't hear a gun? Gus was stabbed?"

"Was he ever. Like about eight times. And practically right in front of the stall, here. Pete knows what happened, eh ol' buddy? Ain't tellin' though. And God only knows what will happen to all of us now. Shit's gonna hit the fan when the owners find out they got no trainer. We shippin' or what?"

"Well, yeah, Meryl says go ahead... Things are settling down, don't worry. Everybody's leaving tomorrow, all signed and sealed. You and Pete don't go till about noon, okay? You go with Tanglefoot, and Meryl's gonna meet you at the airport, everything's fine. And hey, you take advantage of that nice Kentucky air, all right? The change is gonna do you good. You and Tanglefoot, eh? You're a team. You'll come out okay."

"Yeah, I know...we'll be fine. I just feel so sorry for Gus. I known that guy twenty-five years, not a mean bone in his body. Not right at all, this thing, not a bit. And poor Joaquin, he's a wreck... He always had a soft spot fer Gus, y'know. You straighten this out, Jeanie, and you lemme know what the hell is going on, okay?"

I look into his old eyes and swear. "Damn straight, Gabby. I promise you."

* * *

We're home by mid-morning. I give Indy some acetaminophen and tuck her in on the daybed with a video. Zazie and Luke are flying through the apple trees when I come back out. I'm having some trouble breathing, and there's a pain in my chest I can't think about. About every three minutes, I have to check the clock. Having chores to do is a help. Keep going. Don't dwell. Gus was my boss since the dawn of time. No exaggeration, he really *did* teach me everything I know. Grief and panic feel about the same. Breathe, call the kids.

"Which do you guys want to do: keep Indy company, or give me a hand in the barn?"

"I want to *swing* in the trees!" says Zazie.

"Okay, Zaz, but please check on Indy, will you? She'll get lonely."

Zazie swings and flutes, "Okay!"

"Luke, come on, you can help me look for eggs."

I release all the horses into the barnyard first. Luke hikes himself waist high up the fence rail to offer an apple to Frank's black quarterhorse, Dave. The wind lifts Dave's apple-y breath over the fence in a little smelly cloud. Luke rubs the horse's forehead and dangles from the top rail by one arm, chatting. There are seven horses on the place just now: my Sunny, Frank's Dave, three broodmares, and two yearlings I was greenbreaking for Gus. We loaf a minute to look at them. Some things you don't get tired of.

Our two purebreds have earned their keep many times over, getting work in movies and TV shows. Horse wrangling is my winter income, and a crossover into Frank's world that has not so far actually had us both working on the same project.

When there's a showhorse required for some sort of fancy shot, and I don't mean pulling a carriage, we don't do that stuff. But often in a commercial or in a feature film they need a horse who can gallop up, stop on a dime, and turn just so, on the mark, and that's what these guys can do. These horses are camera savvy, I guess would be the way to say it.

Also, film companies don't want to put their stars onto horses who are going to be flipping them up into the bleachers—that's kind of important in the movie world. So, reliability, that's what we do. Our two boys are solid, steady, dear, working horses.

The thoroughbred youngsters are playing at the far

end of the yard, nipping each other, bucking and squealing and generally being kids. Sunny grazes and ignores them. Luke lets himself down and follows the dog as she wags through the long yellow grass at the edge of the fence.

I go into the barn and start mucking the stalls. I'm missing Gus and hurting, and with each shovelful of wet bedding, I'm exorcising, blinking, teeth clamped, loading manure into a wheelbarrow with the strength of misery and outrage, and dumping that on the pile outside. Just keep breathing.

Luke comes in from his wandering and plays awhile in the hayloft. I break open bushels of peat and shake them around each shovelled stall. Zing through the twine on bails of straw and fork the clean yellow stems onto the bedding. As I close the last stall door, finished, Zazie comes in cradling three eggs in her arms. She looks small in the broad stable doorway. I pull off my work gloves, hold her free hand, call Luke down from the loft, and we all walk back to the house.

* * *

By one p.m., the horses are back in their stalls, fed. The mountain of laundry is slightly reduced, the dishwasher emptied, the kitchen floor is washed. The kids have painted several pictures, built a grocery store with Lego, played a couple of rounds of Snap and distributed Barbie clothes evenly over the entire surface of the livingroom floor. They have consumed nourishment, chicken noodle, and toast. Indy is now due for a nap. I answer the phone.

"Doreen, hi, it's nice of you to call." My friend is a stay-at-home mother of four, a steady woman with a really big yard, two miles away near the airport.

"All done at the track, Jean? Ready to gear down to your movie star horses?"

"Whew, I wish. All hell is breaking loose."

"Oh yeah? What?"

"Gus was killed last night."

"What!"

"Oh, God, I know, it's just incredible. And I may be under investigation. My last day at the track was supposed to be yesterday, but I can't leave now. Frank and I are fighting. Indy's feverish. There's only straw left in the hayloft. But everything's okay, there was a can of soup in the cupboard for lunch."

"Hmm," says Doreen. "Think I'll visit you."

"Okay."

I'm putting the phone down, it rings again, it's Frank.

"How's it going, how was it at the track?"

"Everyone is upset, it's very hard on everyone. I think it's going to be really awful for a really long time. Business is squared away, anyhow. How about you?"

"We used the rig, it'll work fine for the shot Dick wants. We met with the rest of the crew for the survey in Maple. We're finished now and just grabbing a bite before we drive back. How's Indy?"

"She's getting sick. She just made it to the end of the job. Now that I've got some time for her, she'll take it. Kids have radar."

"Okay. I'm on my way home. Need anything?"

"Everything. But I'll make a list and go when you get here."

"Okay. See you soon."

I hang up. Why can't I tell him what I need?

I puzzle myself. I pick up the receiver again to call the feed store for a hay delivery.

* * *

Indy's napping. Luke and Zazie are watching *The Princess Bride.*

I'm staring out the window, as I seem to be doing a lot lately. Sitting at the desk in the office, pretending to go over the bookkeeping, but in truth it's just thinking things over, and staring out the window.

All summer we were up by six. The kids were at daycare by seven thirty. Usually Frank had been at work for two hours by then. I got to the track at eight to train a few of our current racers. After that, I'd go to Gus's farm to get on some yearlings, then get home to work with whichever horses I was putting up in our barn. I'd spend some time on the phone with the owners, vets, and blacksmiths. Answer the email, pay the bills, send the faxes, balance the cheque book, issue invoices, move the laundry around, tinker with the windmill generator, repair toys or clothes or kitchen or stable equipment. Replace a window or a solar panel or a fence rail or some roof shingles, pickle cucumbers or put up peaches or make applesauce, run the tractor to grade our track or turn the garden or haul manure, and at three thirty pick up the kids from daycare. We'd play a bit, have supper, feed the livestock and close up the barn. And then I'd run the kids through the bath, and say "hi" to Frank when he came in the door, which was sometimes in time to kiss us goodnight, but usually not.

And what will happen to us now? I had thought I would always have Gus's guidance, his gentle patronage and his friendship, that I'd never lose him. In our last conversation, I'd been such a jerk. I feel terrible about it. I was impatient, and I didn't properly give him his due. Did he know how much I cared about him, valued and trusted him? He was the only solid figure in my life for so many years.

This death was wrong, undeserved in any way. He was a fine person, and dear to me. It's inexplicable. Who could have done this?

I've got that chest thing again, the gasping pain, and I have to check the clock. It's five minutes since the last time I checked the clock. So, it's okay: I couldn't have screwed up in only five minutes.

"Mom!" yells Zazie from the TV room. "Do we have any popcorn?"

* * *

I deliver the popcorn and check the video. It's the part where Vizzini says, "No more rhymes now, I mean it!', and Fezzik says, "Does anybody want a peanut?" Which means it's more than an hour until the end of the movie. Back to the office and my computer, where I should finish updating the records on Gus's racing horses. But halfway into my notes on Rotation, I'm back mooning out the window.

I realize now that I should have been prepared for Gus's reaction when I'd told him I was quitting. How could I have misunderstood his dismay? He had shared with me everything he knew, he'd invested himself in me. I was the heir, for gawdsake! Wow. I thought he was just being stubborn.

He wasn't a stubborn person. He was very flexible,

actually, and particularly accepting of others, though he had ground rules that couldn't be touched. For instance, when I was sixteen, I was breaking yearlings for him at his farm, and most of the time, I was alone there. On a hot afternoon, when the cicadas were screaming, the groom he had working the place at that time had cornered me in one of the stalls. He only scared me. I ran out too quickly for him to lay on a single finger, but I'd told Gus about it, and the groom was gone the next day, replaced. There was to be no harassment under Gus's roof.

Gus had stood up for me a few times over the years. At my wedding. Who else could give me away? Mom had been dead for years, I hadn't seen my dad since I was three, and I had no uncles. There was nobody else. And when I asked him if he would perform this task for me, though I could see his first thought was to run away and hide, he overcame his shyness and gave me a rare hug. "I would be very happy to do this for you, my dear," he said. "I'd be honoured."

Luke comes into the office, and I know it must be the part in the movie where Wesley is being tortured in the Pit of Despair. Hardly anyone's favourite scene. Luke sits on my lap to wait until it's over.

"Whatcha doing, Mom?"

"I'm thinking about Grampa Gus, honey. I miss him."

"Me too. Where did he go?"

"Well, he's not in his body any more. We won't see him again at all, and that makes me really sad. He didn't want to leave us, either, it was a terrible accident."

Luke thinks this over, then his eyes widen with fear.

"Are we going to have a terrible accident too?" he says.

"Nope. Terrible accidents almost never happen. I'm not worried about that part. I just miss Gus."

Luke's face relaxes. We are not afraid, we're just sad. That's cleared up.

The kids saw none of the gruesome evidence at the crime scene this morning, and I didn't tell them about Gus's death until we were back in our car about to go home. They barely understood what I was saying. For them, he's left town. Mortality isn't part of our perspective until so much farther down the line. This news is sinking in slowly, and it's going to take a while.

"Can I have a juicebox, Mom?"

"Sure thing, and take one upstairs for your sister too, would you?"

"Okay."

* * *

Frank and I were married in our living room. Gus looked great in a sky blue silk suit. I had invited my track family, meaning Joaquin, Gabby and Ned, and my neighbour Doreen and her husband Teddy. Frank had invited his daughters, and at the time I thought that was great, it was a good sign to me that he wanted to keep his families together. Later, I thought it was even greater of Rosanne to let them come, to accept me as some part of *her* family, not just some bimbo her ex had knocked up.

Gus was all support, all the time. He believed Frank was a good man, and he helped me feel I was doing the right thing. Before the ceremony, when Doreen had finished helping me get dressed, he came up to my bedroom and tapped on the door. I let him in and he told me I looked great, and he gave me my wedding present, a Passier saddle. I lifted the glossy leather out of his hands to admire the flawless work of this icon of

English saddlemakers, as Gus said, "There's a horse to go underneath, too. He's a little Arab...smart enough for you, Jeanie, and gentle enough for your babies."

That was Grampa Gus.

And at this moment I realize I will have to know who killed Gus, in fairness to him, if I expect to sleep again.

# FIVE

When Frank gets home, I hug him. I've seen his truck pull up, seen him slide out of the cab and stride through the leaves toward the house, his eyes up, his black hair blowing around his cap.

How does he weather his job so well? I love his vitality, the confident look, his straight male energy—irresistible, the capable, independent, sane guy. I want to curl up in his work shirt pocket and hide.

"You look great," I lay my cheek on his chest. He brings his arms around me and rocks a bit, side to side.

"*You're* great. Got a lot on your plate just now, huh, baby." His voice such a comfort, rumbling through his vest. "Tell me about Gus."

I'm not going to cry. I'm "tuff enuff". I break away. "It's nuts. I have no idea what the police found out about the murder, or even if they found out anything. They're giving no information at all—except to suggest maybe I did it." Frank and I exchange a look, our eyebrows up.

"Oh, yeah." I bat my bangs up off my face. Frank has his hand out to touch my cheek, but I make a little motion and duck away. "Meanwhile, the owners are all over the map," I say. Frank is now standing with his arms crossed, he doesn't know where to put them.

I notice my voice is getting louder. "They don't know who to take their horses to. Replace Gus? Or trust Meryl and Joaquin? Grooms don't know if they'll have jobs next week."

Frank's watching me now. I know he's trying to connect with me, but I can't help him. I've fallen into some black hole of miscommunication. "We're just gonna ship as if nothing has happened," I rattle on. "I mean, let the horses run the races they're already entered in. Meryl is handling everything from Louisville. And Joaquin called me, he's got everyone calmed down, and he can go to Kentucky. Thank God, he's not been charged. He'll probably leave after the funeral. Poor guy is heartbroken. Everybody's through the roof."

"And how are you?"

Frank has his hand on my arm.

"Gus may as well have been my father, you know that..."

"And you feel terrible about this."

"I feel terrible about this."

"And you want to know what happened to him."

"And I can't believe it either! It's so nuts! I'm so confused..."

Frank's there, he's standing right there with me, and I know that he loves me. But I can't let go. I can't trust him.

Grow up, Jeanie! Get over it! But I spin away, I turn away, as if I could escape my feelings, and I leave Frank alone in the kitchen.

* * *

I call Doreen and ask her not to come.

"I know it's rude, I'm sorry, I want to see you and I'm so grateful that you would come...but I'm just all in, I'm going to take a nap. Could you possibly make some time for a visit tomorrow? Frank's here. ...afternoon? Great, and bring any kids who want to come? Thank you so much Doreen. ...Yup, we'll talk tomorrow. Thanks...thanks."

Frank goes for the groceries. He brings them home, puts everything away and starts making dinner. Indy and I are on the day bed, under the feather comforter. She's pink with fever, newly dosed with acetaminophen, has just one eye on the TV. I'm holding her on my chest and staring out the window, again.

I met Frank years ago at the track. He was gripping a documentary about racing. I was a novelty then, in the one percentile of women in a male population. For Frank's footage, I had to canter up (and we used a track pony, but who would know it wasn't a racehorse?), rein in and jump off, pull off my helmet, and shake out my hair. You always have to shake out your hair, of course, if you're a girl.

I liked his eyes, and his cheekiness. He was very sweet, and he seemed to think I was absolutely wonderful, and everything I had to say was interesting.

I distrusted every feeling I had with him. I sensed doom. Farm girl meets urbane, divorced, older, upscale boomer, film technician. Clearly a match made in heaven.

Mom was still alive then. When I'd sit to tell her about him, she'd listen to every word, without interruption, chin on her fist. She had married a tough old bird, and it drove her parents nuts when she did. They just hated him. She actually had to buy the farm from them, they were that mad.

Dad was long gone, and Mom's parents in the ground, by the time I was old enough to help her work the place. She pushed herself too hard with work and worry, and when she died, I felt the weight of her determination.

Frank moved in, and renovated. He put up the windmills, put solar panels on the roof of the shed, solar water heaters on the house roof, replaced windows and upped the insulation. He got me growing our vegetables organically and irrigating them with water from rain barrels. He made his own biodiesel fuel for the tractor out of used cooking oil from a local doughnut shop. He was back-to-the-land in a big way. Of course, I'd never left it, and never would. I thought I was the luckiest girl alive.

Frank and I talked about marriage as an adventure. I was scared and thrilled. I wanted a family. Not babies, specifically, but more people, the warmth and wealth of family life, as I hadn't known it. He had two kids already, living with their mom in California, but he said he wanted mine. He seemed so sure about his new life.

It was up to me to see the axe falling, and I watched for it closely. I was afraid I wasn't going to like myself in wedlock, and once committed, I wasn't going to be able to escape. And I knew I'd regret either course, eventually.

So we got ready to marry. But once marriage is announced, it's no longer romance, it's where will all the guests sleep. All my doubts bloomed, my lack of faith rattled Frank, and we started to feel very gloomy about one another.

The wedding date was set back. We agreed without even discussing it. One day I walked into the kitchen where he was seated and said, "Umm, honey? I don't know about this," and Frank just nodded, knew what I meant.

But our mutual uncertainty helped us stay together. It wasn't until two years later, when I was three months pregnant and our futures were irrevocably interwoven, that we finally agreed to have the ceremony.

Mom died much too soon. The kids never got to meet her.

* * *

Luke comes in the room with a cardboard cylinder he's decorated. "See my gun, mom? When I shoot it, people faw down."

"Oh, do they have to fall down, Luke? What if, when you shoot your gun, people can fly? Or feel better?"

"Or, they could have a great idea!"

"Sure, that would be lovely." He leaves and in a little while I hear Zazie's voice, bless her, from her room across the hall.

"I have a great idea!" she says.

Indy's asleep. I get up from the daybed and go downstairs.

Steam clouds the windows and the smells of garlic, olive oil and basil fill the kitchen. Frank's hard at it, and I get my jacket and go out to feed the horses.

* * *

Dave, such a beauty, black and broad, is swishing around in his stall. I put the newly delivered hay in his net. It's herby and fresh, lots of clover and timothy.

Sunny is sleepy, chewing his feed slowly, and the yearlings are kids. They're idiots actually, flat out on their sides already, whew! such a busy day. The mares are thirsty, pressing their muzzles on the automatic water spigots. Their bellies are rounding. Rest your hand on the warm hide and feel the slow movement of little sliding hooves within. This one, Fax Copy, is due in

January, but just now she's concentrating on getting on her winter coat. The new hair is itchy, and I scratch her shaggy backside. Normally, I would ship her back to Gus's farm within the month. I'll have to check with his staff there to see what they want done with her.

A couple of hens are still puttering around, strolling with their little songs. I shuffle them back into the coop, check their grain, close up the henhouse.

Stand outside, it's November, with my breath streaming eastward, winter coming on. I look up at the stars. At Gus.

* * *

Up the drive comes our intrepid Detective Brock.

"Hey there," I say.

"Mrs. Spring, I hope I am not intruding."

"No, please, come inside."

We come into Frank's wonderful kitchen, the pasta in a great bowl beside the stove, as he is dumping on the sauce he's made of tomatoes and zucchini, broccoli flowers, bacon, garlic and cream. My spirits rise.

"Sit with us, please, Detective," I say, as I'm washing my hands. "Kids, Frank, this is Detective Brock. We met today at the track."

"I saw you there!" says Zazie.

"Would you like some of this capellini, Mr. Brock?" Frank, the host.

"Lieutenant. Thank you, no." He turns to me as Frank helps the kids serve themselves at the stove. "Mrs. Spring, could I have a moment of your time."

I have a look at our detective. Wondering what he is here for. Wondering about his formality, his blue windbreaker, and most of all, what does he know about Gus? Were the kids not here, and were it not ridiculous behaviour, I would wrestle him now, to get out what he knows.

"Kids," I say. "Think about this: can you eat for a while, O.Y.O.? That's 'On Your Own'. It's something new I'm working on, it's very cool. Can you handle it?"

Ha ha ha. "Sure, Mommy."

"Frank?..." Tilt my head toward the office.

"Be right there, Jean." The cop and I leave.

"Mrs. Spring, I've spoken with two of the people at the party you say you attended last night. Mr. Richard, or Dick, Dagman, and Ms. Valeria Pura."

I try not to laugh. "You've been interviewing Frank's crew?"

"They confirm that you left the party, with your family, at nine thirty. Could you please tell me what you did after that? And why you lied to me earlier today about where you were?"

I look at Frank, as he comes in the room. He heard the "lied to me" part.

"Detective, I'm not sure what to say to you. You're asking what?"

"Can you establish your whereabouts between nine thirty and midnight last night?"

"I was at home. I got the time wrong before. I was here."

"Mr. Spring, can you confirm this?"

"Sure," Frank begins confidently. "After the wrap party, we came home together. We put the kids to bed, it was, what, Jeanie, close to ten o'clock? And I went to bed then, I was really bagged..."

Frank's voice trails off and he looks at me, thinking.

He realizes he can't help me. He looks away. The detective turns to me.

"Oh, please," I say.

"We have your fingerprints all over the Cadillac, Mrs. Spring," says Lt. Brock.

"Sure, I drive it often, that's nothing to..."

"And we're wondering about your inheritance."

"What?"

"Probate was arranged this afternoon."

"What are you talking about?"

"Mr. Hampton's will. You are one of his beneficiaries. Mr. Hampton left you a lot of money. His wife will keep the residences, the breeding farm in Louisville, the condo in Florida, the share of the hotel in Switzerland. But he left his Toronto place to you. That's a big farm, Mrs. Spring. Barns, a fifteen-room house, his breeding stock, and two hundred acres of fine farmland. You have motive, I must consider you a suspect in his murder."

Thunderstruck, I look over at Frank He's looking at the floor.

"I would never hurt Gus!" I howl.

"You have motive and opportunity, since you cannot prove where you were at the time of the murder," says Detective Brock.

"This is crazy! I...I was here, in my own home!" I'm stuttering, I'm so confused. My stomach has seized, I'm gasping. "I don't need anything from him. There's no motive! I loved Gus. He was always so good to me."

"Why were you leaving Mr. Hampton's employment?"

Frank's head snaps up. "What's that, Jean? What? You were quitting?"

I shoot a look at him. "I was going to tell you about that, Frank. Detective, what could it have to do with anything? What are all these questions? Should I have a lawyer present? Are you arresting me?"

"It would be better for you if you volunteered any information you have in this case."

"I don't *have* any information! Please! If you are not arresting me, I would like you to leave me alone!" I move over toward my husband.

"What the hell is going on, Jean?"

Hey! "Frank, can we have just one interrogation at a time here, please?"

He looks me in the face for a second, and then relaxes slightly, and turns to Brock. "Detective, she's right. What are you hoping to achieve here? My wife was very fond of Gus, and very shaken by his death."

Zazie slips her hand into mine. I've not seen her come in, but no way would she miss this. She's staring hard at the detective. He is aware of his audience.

"All right, Mrs. Spring, I'll see myself out. But yes, you should speak with your lawyer."

# SIX

When Brock has left, we collapse in the kitchen. I've got shock symptoms: fluttery pulse, lightheadedness and nausea. Zazie sits on my lap and looks me in the eye.

"Why was...what did he... Mom? What was that?"

"Honey, I'm confused too," I say, pulling in a breath. Frank gets busy at the sink. Indy and Luke haven't touched their dinner.

"He thinks you killed Grampa Gus?" Nothing escapes her.

"Whoa. How nuts is that, eh, Zaz?"

"Way nuts, Mom."

"Yeah, way nuts. What are you doing there, Frank?"

"Oh, just tidying up," he says, without turning.

"You kids not hungry?"

'My throat is sore, Mom."

"Poor Indy, you don't look very well either."

"I'm hungry for crackers and jam!" enthuses Luke.

"Crackers only after dinner, Lukie." I look at Zazie. "And we're not hungry, are we sweetie," I say. "Well, this has been a pretty crazy day. You guys do what you like. It's a great capellini, Frank. Thanks for your trouble. I'm sure we'll enjoy it some other time."

"Sure, maybe even just later tonight," he rallies. Luke takes a banana and drifts out of the room with Indy. Zazie hops off my lap and sits down to eat everything on her plate. Don't try to pin her down, by golly.

We have broad industrial shades on the two lamps that hang down from the ceiling, low over the kitchen table. They give a nice soft light, and when it's dark outside, as it is now, the lights reflect on the big triple-glazed picture windows across the back of the house. I get up and close the insulation curtains. In daylight, you can see through these south-facing windows into the ravine, see the creek down there, the woods and the pastureland. See our two windmills up here on the ridge, where there's always a wind blowing. When the winter sun shines, we get enough passive solar heating from this wall of glass that we don't need the furnace.

Zazie finishes her supper, flips down her fork and leaves the kitchen. Frank sits down with me.

"You quit your job?" he says.

"I've been thinking about it for a long time."

"You didn't tell me you were thinking about it."

"We never seem to have a chance to talk."

"You were going to wait until I noticed you were unemployed?"

"It wasn't spite, Frank. I was unsure about the whole thing, and it didn't even seem real until yesterday. Gus offered to send me to Churchill Downs, instead of Joaquin."

"Wow. Nice offer."

"Yeah. But you know how when you toss a coin, you finally know which way you wanted it to fall? I can't take Gus's promotion. Leave you and the kids and follow the racing season around the continent? Not for me."

"No. You wouldn't leave your farm."

"No. But I can't keep on at the track here just the same either. I...started thinking about it after that fall last month."

"You've been dropped off so many times, Jean. Hell, you've fallen off every horse you ever rode."

"Practically," I agree.

"I didn't know that particular fall was special."

"Well, it turns out it was really special." I'm looking at Frank's straight shiny black hair and his straight blue gaze at me. "I don't feel safe anymore. I can't ride anymore, really."

He absorbs this and leans back in his chair. "So you've quit racing."

"Have to."

He taps his fork on his plate. "It's going to leave a bit of a gap in your life, Jean."

"And Gus has been murdered."

"And I'm not talking to my husband," Frank says.

"No, I'm not talking to my husband, though he's a great guy."

"He's a great guy, and you have a thousand things on your mind."

"I have a thousand things on my mind, and my heart is broken."

"Your heart is broken, and you just can't talk."

"I just can't talk, and my friend is dead."

"Your friend is dead, and you feel responsible."

I sob aloud, it just pops out.

"That's it, that's it: I feel responsible. I should have protected him." This hopeless truth pierces me. I sit back in my chair, and tears roll down. Frank has helped me over a hurdle in my grief.

"Turn your back for one second," he shakes his head and winks at me.

"And all hell breaks loose." I grin back.

In the bleakest moments, humour.

After a moment, Franks continues. "But there's more, eh, Jeanie."

"What."

"Gus left you his farm."

I gasp, cover my face with my hands, breathless in disbelief. "I'd honestly put this out of my mind," I say. "I just don't know what to do with this information. I don't know how I feel, apart from baffled, and undeserving, and uprooted.

"It's going to take me a while to get used to this, Frank. I didn't want anything more from Gus; he'd already given me so much. What the hell do we need with another farm, anyway? It's just unthinkable."

We clean up the dinner dishes and put the kids through their bedtime routine. Indy bathes peacefully, alone, in deep bubbles, then puts on a fresh nightie and settles under her duvet without hesitation. Zazie and Luke then pour a clear bath, the better to see marine life, underwater tractors, surface speedboats. Megazord and Godzilla battle furiously, and action figures enact heroic rescues and daring flips off high diving towers. A four towel bath, two for the kids, two to wipe up the floor.

"Now, I wonder if you guys can show me which clothes your Barbies need tonight? And the rest we can fold for tomorrow."

Will they perceive the hidden intent of cleaning up the mess in the livingroom? No! They scramble downstairs. In another year, at the most, it won't be this easy.

We dress dollies for a while, and then change the Lego store into two airplanes that make a lot of noise diving and landing, with passengers getting off and on, and Frank shows us how to Go On Vacation, a really good game with customs officials and airplane food and dollies who wear swim fins. Eventually, it's all put away, the teeth are brushed, the hairs are dry, the lights are out and the parents on their own.

* * *

"So who do you think killed Gus?" We're in our room, folding laundry.

"Wait a second. Can't you let the police solve this, Jean?"

"Are you kidding? They think I did it! They haven't got a clue who murdered him."

"So you're going to figure it out?"

"Well, I feel like I have to. As long as I'm still not in jail anyway. I've got to find a lawyer in the morning. Our guy practices only family law. Jesus!" I sock my forehead. "Should I be planning to get someone to look after the kids? I feel like I'm going to get swallowed up in the maw of the legal system. This is scary!"

Frank says, "Do you know a criminal lawyer? Does anyone we know?"

I barely hear him, I skip over his question. "If I am arrested… Well, we could make bail anyway, eh? We could put the farm up as collateral."

Frank stops folding and sits down on the corner of the bed. He's got his mouth tight up against one side. "Jean, sit down here, I gotta tell you something."

"Sure, okay Frank."

"When it came out today that you had been dealing with your decision about work, about your future, by yourself, I felt terrible."

"I should have brought it up with you, honey," I say quickly. "It's a big deal for me, but it affects you too, very much. I was wrong not to discuss it with you. And I'm really glad that it's out in the open now. I feel like a barrier between us has dropped."

"Well, that's not all I wanted to say."

"Okay, I'm braced." I smile at him encouragingly.

"I felt bad about your isolation with this difficult problem, but I also felt sort of...glad."

"Hmm. Glad about what?" I sit down beside him.

"I have a secret too, and I felt better about having this secret when I found out that you also had one."

"Ah-hah, equality..." I think about this for a minute and jump to a conclusion. "I'm not having an affair, Frank."

"No! I'm not having an affair either, Jean! No...this is about the farm. At the moment, I guess this is going to sound pretty terrible, though at the time it seemed like a wonderful idea."

"Shoot, Franklin." No more smiling.

He glances at the ceiling, then back to me. "Dick has a film property which looks absolutely incredible. It's a fantastic script. It's cast already, big names were practically fighting each other to get into this movie... He was looking for financial backing in order to go into production. It's just *this* far from being greenlit."

"This isn't possible," I interrupt. The blood has drained from my head, I can't breathe.

"I'm Key Grip *and* Producer, for godssake, on a really fine movie, something with *meaning*, about what's important in a moral sense. A film we can be proud of, that will probably also make a lot of money..."

"You mortgaged my farm."

"Sort of."

"You thieved my farm to make a moral movie."

"I knew you'd feel uncomfortable with it, Jean..."

"I can't believe you would do this. I can't lose this farm."

"It's not like the farm is at risk, really. This is practically a sure thing."

"This should never have happened. Your instinct was correct: I never would have agreed to this."

"A wonderful surprise, like a winning lottery ticket."

"If I'm arrested, we have no bail money."

"This is an event I did not foresee."

"And when Brock looks into our financial picture, we're going to appear to be strapped, mortgaged to the hilt, and desperate. I'll appear to have a motive to kill Gus, to get his money."

Frank puts his arm over my shoulders, and we sit together quietly for a minute.

"Gus chose a terrible time to be murdered," he says.

I hit him with some folded jeans. "Quit it! Don't attempt to worm your way back into my affection, you creep! You have made a huge mistake here, buster, apart from your terrible timing."

"I appreciate that. I'm sorry. I made a terrible mistake."

"Damned straight you did. EEE!" I shriek. "You're very frustrating to me, Frank! You help me in so many ways, and with my feelings about Gus, but then you screw up our finances! That was so hair-brained!"

He's meek, dammit. It's very perplexing.

"It's not as if you can't afford it, now," he says quietly.

"YUCK! That's horrible!" I recoil from him. "What a horrible thought! You've taken my farm and now you're all over Gus's farm too! Oh, I hate this!"

He gazes at me like I'm exactly the berserk woman I am. "That's unreasonable, Jeanie," he says. "That's not what I was saying. Okay, look, you've had a terrible day, a few terrible days. Just try to calm down, will you. We need a good sleep and some perspective."

I clamp my mouth shut, naked in my thoughts.

In our bed, the night ticks quietly by. Awake beside my irresponsible husband, I go over my options. Law suit? Do I have to divorce him to get my farm back? Who *is* this guy? How can he *sleep?*

How could the bank have approved the mortgage without me? Forgery? I feel I'll burst; I haven't room for all this anguish. Gus's murder, the ludicrous blame the police want me to concede, and Frank's betrayal. I can barely breathe...

# SEVEN

I jerk awake. It's dark. Frank is sleeping, the window is open, the curtains are flowing. Someone has called.

I get out of bed and trot down the hall to the girls' room. Indy is coughing with a heavy, weary congestion that doesn't clear. In the glow of her cartoon nightlight, I find her face to feel. She's very hot, breathing in shallow puffs as quick as heartbeats, her lungs making a wheezing sound at each exhalation.

"Okay, sweetie, better sit up. I'll be right back." I get pillows from the daybed, chewable acetaminophen and liquid ventolin from the bathroom. Indy chews the tablets, and I arrange the pillows so she can relax almost upright. "So, how do you feel. Anything hurt?"

"No, I'm fine, Mom." Her voice sounds so normal. We pretend there's nothing wrong.

"Good. Well, just relax, and the medicine will look after your fever in a little while. Do you think you could sleep in this position?" Indy settles her shoulders into the pillows, nods. She's struggling for each breath.

"Here, Duck. This one's for your lungs. Close your eyes a sec." I flip on the light so I can measure the bronchodilator into a teaspoon and turn it off so she can see to take the medicine. I get a cold cloth and put it on her forehead, then sit by the bed. "There you go. Just think about palm trees now." I'm getting cold. I think about palm trees too. I hold Indy's fiery little hand. She gives me a squeeze and a grin from under the facecloth.

Since their premature birth, the lungs have been the twins' weak spot. We've been through this before. Zazie is sleeping soundly in her top bunk. I won't wake Frank unless Indianna gets worse: he has to get up for work in about three hours anyway. I run down to our room to get my housecoat and get comfortable beside Indy. I'm thinking about my babies.

Pregnancy is nine months long because you need at least that much time to get used to the idea. *Pregnant? POW!* Whether thrilled or appalled, you sure collect your jaw up off the floor.

I was twenty-five, self-supporting, an athlete. Late in the racing season I began feeling unaccountably queasy and lightheaded. My breasts hurt, I'd missed a period. We were delighted at the positive pregnancy test. I pictured myself continuing to train from the ground, the baby strapped to my back. We agreed to marry, radiant with pleasure at the change in our dynamic.

Pregnancy is a time of gradual transition. Nature, marvellously and relentlessly, shuffles you along from one hormone to the next and leads you to accept having your life overhauled. Babies change everything. No one can be prepared for how completely babies change everything.

In the first three months, my body rang with demands. I had to eat every couple of hours or faint. I was weak and easily upset, I fell asleep every night at eight, woke up every morning with what felt like flu. I became fascinated by new topics: protein diets, home redecorating, birthing practices of tribal Asians.

In the second trimester, I got a little break, where I was neither too barfy nor too huge to enjoy myself. I had lots of energy, and I'd figured out where the baby would sleep; I had the world by the tail. Gradually, my body helped me to accept change: slowing my walk, waking me from time to time in the night, moving me into new wardrobes. I was provided with physical tics that my obstetrician and midwife could discuss with me. Everything was falling into place.

Twins were diagnosed in the fifth month, February. By mid-March I was alarmed at my predicament, because I was enormous, and everything hurt. I couldn't ride, I'd get cramps just walking to the barn. My breasts leaked. I had to get out of bed to roll over. We were not to have sex, it might start labour. My body had deserted me, off on a course of its own. And I had debts—I was no longer going to be able to pay my share of our expenses. Financial reliance on Frank scared me. I wasn't just having a baby, now, I was a high risk pregnancy, a walking incubator, all my food the purest nutrition, all my pleasures restricted. Eventually, if I didn't stay quietly in my own bed, I'd be hospitalized.

I felt threatened and outnumbered, and, unfairly, I felt abandoned by Frank. He was anxious about his changing responsibilities too, distant and cranky. He must have wondered about getting into all this stuff again, losing his girlfriend to the baby onslaught. He'd maybe forgotten what it was like. He had lots of casual professional pals, but nobody really close. For friends, I was it, and I was busy.

This was my first child, and I didn't know what to expect. I couldn't manage on my own. I needed Frank, but I was prideful and stubborn. He'd been through this before, he knew about it, and I didn't. It took away from my adulthood, somehow, to ask him for his experience.

Not the tuff modern woman. I didn't want him to know how I felt. So we remained isolated from each other, concealed. You hardly ever need help when you're feeling well enough to ask for it.

Frank juggled his filming schedule to attend birthing classes. He wanted to be involved. Birth coaches are supposed to take control for the person who can't find hers. I didn't like the practice sessions, Frank telling me when I could breathe, yelling at me about my focus. Like he was trying to control *me.* So I was uncooperative. I mean, I ignored him. He felt like an idiot. Also, I wondered if he was more interested in the babies than in me. I was jealous of the unborn and deeply resentful at how powerless I felt.

However, I also felt happier than I could ever remember. I was fulfilled, cosmic, ethereal. A biological bliss lifted me. I was astonished, absorbed, at peace, dazzled. I turned in, away from Frank.

I marvelled to feel the babies moving inside my body. What mother can forget this wonderous pleasure? I stroked my stomach and dreamed of the tiny clenched hands, the dear faces, the small people I would cuddle and adore and for whom I would change the world.

Frank was peripheral, but game for the adventure. It's very hard to buck nature. In bed, he lay eye-level with my huge stomach and sang lullabies. He matched my weight gain, pound for pound. He indulged my food cravings (chocolate ice cream), rubbed my back, mucked stalls and scrubbed the bathtub when I no longer could. He told me I looked beautiful.

Change, fear, grumbling, euphoria. Pregnancy is scary; and also an unfounded, untouchable optimism. This is nature's gift.

* * *

Early, the metamorphosis was over.

"This is odd," I said to Frank. We were sitting in the hospital outside my obstetrician's office, awaiting my weekly check-up. "I have to breathe right through these contractions now."

I'd been having spasms for two days, but they were weak and irregular, and I hadn't thought much about them. Just experiencing a little pressure, I told my doctor, maybe gas.

He listened to my story, checked my cervix, and told me to stay on the table.

"You're a wise guy, huh?" he said, his face white. He ordered a wheelchair. "I'm going to try to stop your labour."

Apparently, women hardly ever know when they're in labour. Having had it, you can't believe anyone could miss it, but people do. It's one of nature's little tricks. Every labour is different, and it's just hard to tell. We'd wanted a natural childbirth, no drugs, no fuss.

"You're five centimeters dilated," he declared. "It's a free country, you can walk out of here if you like, but those babies are going to be born in about an hour and a half, and they're too premature to survive it."

Oh. Well, if you put it that way.

So I was wheeled up to the maternity floor, I.V. attached to the hand, shot of cortisone in the hip. If labour stopped in response to the muscle relaxant, vasodalin, I could have a stitch put in my cervix and be restricted to this hospital bed for four or five weeks, until the due date.

* * *

Indy fidgets, slips sideways off her pillows in her light sleep. Her breathing rasps faster and louder in this new position. I try to straighten her up again. Not sure if she's awake, I whisper: "Would you like some water, honey?"

"Yes, please, Mom," Indy answers clearly, fully conscious. I hurry to get it for her. She drinks some and puts the half-full cup on the ledge by her bed. She can reach it if she needs it. She settles back, satisfied. Her bravery is so touching: she feels in control now that she can reach her own water. She's all there, a full person, handling an emergency. How can this be? She's only six years old.

"I love you very much, Indianna Spring," I murmur, smoothing her hair in the dark. Indy leans over and hugs me with her thin arms.

* * *

The night slips by, heavy branches outside waving slowly in the wet wind. When the babies were tiny, still having their four a.m. feeding, I loved this solitude, this time that was just ours. The twenty-four hour life.

The morning after the Caesarean, I woke early, no longer pregnant, and alone in my room. The operation was a dream to me, I was very disoriented, and depressed: my body was telling me the babies had died. Governed by hormones and shock and modern medicine, I couldn't stop crying. At five thirty that morning, I called Frank: "Dear, are you coming soon?"

When he came, we got a wheelchair to carry me to the nursery where the babies were sleeping. They were fine, healthy, but so tiny and unavailable, I felt swamped by a sense of lonely tragedy. Here were two new people, who knew no one in town but us. I'd never known what vulnerability and heartache were before that moment.

Frank and I were partners then, we had to be, we were on our hands and knees with fatigue for the first while. At that time, we were trying to nurse the babies and also give supplementary bottles of formula. They'd nurse for about a half hour, then take almost as long to drink two ounces of Similac. Close to an hour for Indy, another hour for Zaz. Then we'd sleep for an hour, or rush around and do laundry, or tear off to do errands, or feed ourselves. Then Indy would wake up hungry. We had this schedule all spring.

Sometimes it seemed like the nicest thing I could do for Frank, one of the few things I could do for him, exhausted as we were, was to let him sleep. I'd take an extra turn with the babies, whatever. But when I started protecting him like that, I also started blocking him out, pushing him away from us. Eventually, it was as if I had taken the babies with me into a cave and rolled a rock up against the door. I was utterly absorbed by them. They had a frowzy, gently electric feel, small beings big with life, growing as I watched. They'd beam at me, focus their little glow on me, murmuring from behind their bottles, dark eyes dancing.

Frank had to go back to work. Then, there was no one to talk to at home.

* * *

Indy's breathing is slow and smooth. She's wiggled down off most of the pillows, but it seems to be okay. I tiptoe back to bed. Frank's alarm will give us news of the outside world in about twenty minutes.

# EIGHT

Here's one: 'We Will Defend You Aggressively'. Yeah, that's what I want," I say. Frank and I are prickly with each other, but we are not fighting. I don't think either of us knows what to say. We are at the kitchen table with coffee and the Yellow Pages. It's daybreak, and I have to find a lawyer. Mostly awake, I continue scanning the ads. "Unfortunately, these guys will only defend me aggressively if I have slipped and fallen and have a brain injury. The theme that I'm noticing is they don't defend murderers in the Yellow Pages." It's premature to mention the divorce litigators I was thinking about a few hours ago.

"You must have bumped into lots of lawyers around the track, Jeanie," Frank says. "Racehorse insurance claims, racing accidents and personal injury claims, million dollar horse sales..."

"True, but all the ones I know are Gus's lawyers. I don't think they're gonna rush out to rescue his assassin."

"Hmm. Well, the guy who handled your mom's estate would know somebody."

Through the ceiling above us we hear Zazie's heels hitting the floor of her room, and faintly, her voice.

"It's mor-ning!" she trills. Thud-thud-thud she flat-foots down the stairs and into the kitchen. She looks odd: her neck is swollen up under her earlobes.

"Hey there, Miss Girl. Lemme feel you." She comes

over, pleased, and I cover her forehead with my palm. "Yup, maybe 101 degrees here."

Frank salutes her. "Congratulations, you have joined the Legion of the Sick."

"Take a seat, my dear—no school today for you."

"I'd like pancakes, Mom," she says, climbing onto her chair. Our Zazie: alert, careless, impulsive, beaming girl. By fever her head is bloodied, but unbowed.

"Another wonderful day begins," says Frank, pulling on his jacket.

"How long is this job, Mr. Rock Video?" I say, handing Zazie a cup of juice.

"Today's in a house, and it'll be long because we have to get it all in one day. Then Tuesday is the gravel pit." He hugs me, and holds on for a minute. "You okay?"

I feel a hundred ways, but okay is in there somewhere. "Yup," I tell his down-filled collar. "Joaquin will handle the shipping at the track. I'll phone a lawyer. Swing by the pediatrician with Indianna. And Doreen's visiting this afternoon."

"Okay. I'll rustle up some suspects."

"Wonderful." I let him go. He gives Zazie a kiss on the cheek and goes outside through the mudroom.

I turn to Zazie's flushed, cheerful face. Let the day begin, indeed.

"First, for you, something for that fever. And you need your slippers. And I've got to check on your sister. C'mon upstairs and hop on the couch, buttercup."

"But, pancakes..."

"I'll bring 'em up in a bit. Here, take your apple juice with you."

I meet Luke in the hall as he's coming out of his room. Sleepy, he droops on my leg and aims kisses softly at the floor. In spite of her rough night, Indy is up, trailing around in her housecoat. I herd everyone into the den and onto the daybed. Bring the pillows back from Indy's room, pull comforters out of the closet, dole out acetaminophen. *Sesame Street* is on, hurray. Go downstairs, drink coffee.

Shall I be a superb parent today? Grief is very near, like the air in the room. I'm tired from sitting up night after night, but in a way I feel limitless too, no borders, no small stuff. As the pancakes brown in the frying pan, I compose a breakfast tray: juice, raisins, syrup, apple and orange slices.

I hear them upstairs. Big Bird says, "A! B! C!" The girls say, "A! B! C!" Lukie says, "No! C is *my* favourite!" Zazie says, "Lukie, don't hit." They are a whole lot more in focus than I am. I carry the tray upstairs, and we all snuggle, eat, stare. At seven thirty, I call the pediatrician's answering service to get on the list for a morning consult. He responds within the hour and hearing the symptoms, tells me what time to come to his office. Indy gets another dose of bronchodilator, and we start a pegasus puzzle. I call the school to say the girls will be absent. Put the phone down, it rings.

"*Ola*, Jeanie, how you doing, *muchacha*?"

"Hey Joaquin, how are you, you poor dear. Are you at the track?" I get up off the couch and go into the hall to talk.

"Yes, I am here, we are packing. I am a wreck, that is for sure, but we are getting this job done pretty good now, *chica*. Everybody is getting out of here on schedule."

"Way to go, tiger. So, what's going on? Are the police still there? Has that guy Brock spoken with you?"

"Police are here, yes. Yellow tape is everywhere. And the detective, he spoke, sure. We talk a long time together. He has concluded that I did not kill Gus."

"No kidding."

"Right, yes."

"He was here, you know, asking me where I was at the time, and all that. He scared me. Like he was going to arrest me."

"He want to interrogate you 'cause you so cute, *querida*."

"That was it. What did he ask you?"

"Oh, like, what Gus and me were arguing about, who do I think kill him, that sort of thing."

"What *were* you arguing about, anyway? And who did kill him?"

"Like I was telling to the detective, I was arguing with Gus about this very thing. I think what happened to our Gus is Mason Goddart kill him."

"That guy is back around? That's bad news."

"Yes, I seen him. Do you remember, oh, seven, eight years ago, he claimed that colt off Gus..."

"I do remember. Gus was crazy about that horse, and no wonder, he was a fine colt. And one of the first horses Gus had bred, too, wasn't he? Goddart got him in a claiming race for something ridiculous, a few grand I think, right?"

"That is him. Gus was so disappointed, but that's racing, eh, *chica*? Goddart got lucky. Lost the horse himself sometime later, though, and his luck went downhill from there. Horse did well out west, though."

"I heard that too. So what about Mason Goddart?"

"Guy's a bum. Gambling debts, people coming after him, he comes to Gus for a favour. Says he has no one else to turn to. You know what that means."

"Burned all his bridges."

"Right, yes. Gus still has a little resentment, but you know him, he is willing, and he loans him money. This was last May, I remember it 'cause it was the same day as the Kentucky Derby. We are on our way to your house to watch the race on TV."

"So Goddart was hitting on Gus for gambling money."

"Could be, yes. Anyway, this month, Goddart is around again. And Saturday in the parking lot, I am saying to Gus, don't you give this guy another cent, you aren't helping him, you know what I am saying, Jeanie?"

"You think Goddart killed Gus for the cash in his jacket? Oh, God."

"He's mean enough to do this, Goddart. So I tell the detective all about my idea, and how I know Gus give him money last spring, and how I see Goddart hanging around again now, like a vulture. But I don't know if Gus say he would give more money to him or what. I am thinking, if Gus do as I say, refuse Goddart, and Goddart kill him... I wish I was with Gus that night."

This conversation is getting into some very painful stuff. It's a terrible burden Joaquin feels might be his.

"Oh, man," comes out of me like a groan. "This is awful. Please don't blame yourself, honey, your advice was not wrong. This isn't your fault."

"He was a sweet guy, our Gus."

"You were so good for him. He had his best years with you."

"That was mutual."

We think about that for a minute. Then I say, "When did you see the detective, Joaquin?"

"That same night, Saturday. They pick me up right

from the parking lot, keep me at the station till morning, talking."

"Poor you! You've been having a horrible time."

"Not as bad as Gus," he says quietly. "Poor guy, alone, dying in his car."

"You're a brave one, my dear."

"Yes, sure. I am shipping horses now, *muchacha*."

"Funeral's day after tomorrow?"

"At the Holy Trinity downtown, yes."

"I'll see you then, Joaquin." I go reeling back into the den and check my watch. "All right, you guys, I gotta pop out and feed the horses, and then it will be time to go see Dr. Jack. So will you start getting yourselves ready? Zazie, get dressed please, and give Luke a hand getting his clothes on? Indy, want to take some books along with us?"

"I don't want to go to see Dr. Jack!" asserts Zazie.

"Sure, I'll pick some," agrees Indy. "I want *Leo the Late Bloomer, Outside Over There* and *Alfie Gets In First.*"

"Good choices. And put on some warm clothes, eh, Indy."

"I'd yike a scram-bowed eggy, Mom," admits Luke, standing up.

"We're finished with breakfast now, big boy. Zazie's going to help you put your pants on."

"I'm not sick! I don't have to go to the doctor!" repeats Zazie.

"He'll just take a peek down your throat, Zaz, no big deal. Sweater, please."

And so on. When I get back in from the barn, everyone is dressed, then soon strapped in the car. When I was little and sick, my pediatrician made house calls, a big advantage over this drafty car ride with feverish children. But Dr. Jack has been a steady ally through these years, always available to me by phone in his bright west-end office, jolly and non-threatening to the kids, and a careful diagnostician.

Indy sits on my lap, and Luke swings his feet beside his sister on the examining table. Zazie calls her doctor by his first name, Jack, and in the car has drawn a picture for him to put on his wall. He talks to her about it while he feels her neck. He checks Zazie's ears, chatting with her, and looks down her throat, makes a note on her chart. He nods to me and winks: she's okay. He tickles her lightly, she giggles and starts to put on her shirt.

Indy is not so charmed by Dr. Jack, but she lets him peer into her ears and listen to her chest. His patter stops, we got trouble.

"Her lungs are quite congested, Jeanie," he observes quietly. "You're giving her ventolin at home?"

"She needed it last night."

"I can switch you to another bronchodilator, possibly an antibiotic as well, for what it's worth. If these don't work, however, there'll be no other treatment outside hospital. She could come in for a ventolin tent overnight, that might do the trick."

"I'd rather keep her at home, if I could try that route," I say, using as neutral a tone as possible.

"Fine." He turns to write the prescription. "There'll be side effects to this medication, hyperactivity, possibly nausea. Phone me later to let me know how she's doing. All right, Indy?" He pats her shoulder and turns to Luke. "And what are you doing here, young man? Do you have the same cold as your big sisters?"

"No way!" he dismisses, hopping down off the table. "I not sick!" Luke swings open the door and leaves.

Jack lifts his eyebrows and laughs. "I see! Bye then! And, Jeanie...call me."

* * *

Seventy-eight dollars later, I've filled the prescriptions and the twins are back in bed. Luke is redistributing a pile of leaves under the apple trees. The good spirits Indy showed this morning, while we did puzzles, are gone. The car trip has exhausted her, the medication is turning her stomach. She falls asleep immediately in her bed, puffing with a sound like boiling water. Zazie sings to herself awhile and dozes off in her top bunk.

It's eleven thirty. I'm in the office at the front of the house, with an eye on Luke out the window. I have two phone calls to make.

"Hi, Doreen, it's me."

"Hello, Jean. Do we still have a plan today?"

"I'm sorry, I'm going to have to cancel again. Both the girls are sick now."

"Oh, dear."

"We went to the doctor this morning and he feels Indy is getting quite serious. Zazie's not feeling too bad, it's just a virus and it'll pass, but I've got to keep Indy quiet and really watch her."

"I was going to say," Doreen reflects, "that since the kids have been playing together all week, they probably have the same cold anyway, no risk of infecting each other if they visit today. But I know what you mean. When they start to get really sick, it's another matter. What are her symptoms?"

And so on, in the way that mothers of small children share information about an illness. Doreen is sympathetic, but she also wants to know what to watch for in her own daughter, and how quickly this could spread through her four kids.

"So, what's the latest with the murder investigation?"

"Oh, God, I don't know. The detective was here last night."

"Yike."

"He said I had lied about where I was at the time of the murder, and that I had reason to kill Gus. He practically threatened me with arrest. It was scary. The stress! Gus's death alone is huge, but that someone wants to blame me for it... I feel like I must deserve this somehow. Maybe I *am* a felon. I'm almost grateful that the kids are sick, I can hide away with them and avoid this whole thing. I'm supposed to get some legal representation, but I can't get myself to make the call."

"You're tired out, my dear. You can't think straight if you're exhausted. Remember that you feel terrible because you have lost your friend and remind yourself that you are innocent of his death. Call someone to get the process of your defense underway then get some sleep. Where is your husband?"

"Working. He'll be home." I don't want to tell her about his deceit. I don't know what I would say. "Thank you, Doreen. You are my very good friend, and you are completely right. I will follow your advice exactly."

"Good girl. Call me when you want to."

* * *

Okay, I can do this. The lawyer.

"Mr. Akerman, hi, it's Jeanie Spring. You were executor of my mother's estate—she was Margo Cassidy?"

"Yes, Mrs. Spring, sure, your farm's out on Indian Line. How can I help you."

"I'd like your advice finding a criminal lawyer. I don't

know where to start to find someone to, uh, represent me."

"Actually, you may not know, our firm does handle quite a range of litigation. What sort of legal action are you involved in?"

"Well, there's been a, uh, a murder, Mr. Akerman, and the police have been asking me, uh, have indicated that I might do well to... But I just don't know where to begin on this. Perhaps you could tell me...what people do, usually, when they are being questioned in connection with, ah...murder?"

He is quiet and I have a mortified opportunity to picture him at his desk, fresh white shirt, silk tie, smooth hair properly combed and parted on the side, gold cufflinks winking, everything about him composed, principled and authoritative.

"I have the name of someone here, Mrs. Spring," he says finally. "Carla Madison is a very fine defence lawyer and a good person as well. She will help you clear up this misplaced investigation straight away." He gives me her phone number.

"Thank you, Mr. Akerman, very much," I say, writing it down, hugely relieved at his compassionate response.

"No problem at all. If you like, tell Carla that I gave you her number. I'm sure she'll clear some time for you right away."

I call Ms. Madison and briefly describe my situation. She suggests I come to her office Wednesday afternoon. I make the appointment for after the funeral, but she tells me to call her if I need to before then.

So that's it, I'm ready for the onslaught.

# NINE

Zazie wakes up hungry. Luke comes in fresh-cheeked from the yard with the dog, both of them panting and beaming, apple leaves in their hair, the boy ready for lunch. I give the kids grilled cheese sandwiches and go upstairs to check on Indy. She's still sleeping, but her breathing is less ragged and her fever is down. I praise antibiotics. Homeopathy has its place, by god, but antibiotics are a mother's friends.

When she finally wakes from her nap, she is feeling better. She eats a tiny serving of Frank's leftover capellini. I spread some stickerbooks on the kitchen table so each child can invent a story using the colourful vinyl figures on the glossy playboards. Zazie puts Sharon, Lois and Bram on the tape machine and we sing along. That combo—sticker sets and music—is good for at least half an hour.

On the corner of the table, I take a pad of paper and begin a list of all the people I know who knew Gus. I think about each of them and speculate upon their innocence. The list of people at the track goes like this:

Joaquin: Gus's long-time friend and assistant trainer. A decent man, soulful and loyal: stop right there, no way he did it.

Meryl: The other assistant, newer to the team, just came on last spring, so I know him less well. This hardly condemns him; he seems a good guy, and I never saw any conflict between him and Gus.

Gabby: Been with Gus forever, loves him like a son. An excellent groom, knows horses backwards, getting a bit dottery but absolutely not a violent person.

Tanglefoot: Not the brightest light on the porch, one of those guys that falls out of some penniless drifting past, finds he likes horses, and holes up on the shed row. A good heart, however. I trust him with Luke, for chrissake.

Phil and Irene: Our married couple. Gus was their boss, landlord and sheriff, and the horses are their kids. Eccentric but solid.

Ned: The exercise boy. Well, Ned went to hospital Saturday morning—that's a pretty good alibi.

I think about the owners. Gus was training about three dozen racehorses, and managed a score of studs and breeding mares. Did the owner of any of these horses feel Gus had mishandled his investment?

Or did Gus owe some terrible debt; was he a closet gambler? Was he in trouble legally somehow, fraud or blackmail or smuggling? And was any of it awful enough to get murdered for? How could someone keep such a secret? Would his lawyers know anything? How do people find out about this stuff? Damn! This is not at all my area of expertise.

"If you were vegetarian," Luke tells Indy, "you could eat hot dogs. Hot dogs are pee-ants."

"They are NOT plants, Lukie, they don't GROW," corrects Zazie. Indy is beginning to look a bit run down again.

"Indy, my dear, are you ready to get back to bed? You could watch a movie."

"Okay, Mom. I'd like *Finding Nemo*."

Drop everything. Zazie and Luke thud-thud-thud up the stairs, and Indy and I follow at a sedate pace. The siblings make a place for her, and she settles on the daybed while I find the video. "Kids, I'm going to take this chance to muck the stalls. Call me on the intercom if you need to, okay? Kids?" I have to repeat a couple of times, because they are already giggling at the movie, but finally my voice gets through, and I can go off to collect my thoughts.

* * *

The horses are anxious to get outside, and they neigh at me when I open the barn door. I lead each one to the paddock to bounce around while I fork out the worst of the mess in the stalls and shake on some fresh straw.

How can I find out about Gus's associates? I thought I knew everyone he knew, but I didn't think about the person Joaquin fingered, this Mason Goddart guy. With such abundant variables, I'd have to stay with what I know, and keep poking at that until something pops up.

A detail that keeps nagging, for instance, is Gus's last minute offer to send me to Kentucky to train in Joaquin's place. What was he thinking? That's a big change for everybody. And where does that leave Meryl? Was Gus moving him elsewhere, or letting him go? I must ask both men about this.

I've got a filly on the shank walking to the paddock. It's three o'clock, the time of day that Gus often used to show up to check how I was doing. His Cadillac would bump up our long driveway, and Marilyn would bark her head off.

"Well, Jeanie, how are my fillies?" He would yell at me,

typically, from the driver's seat.

In my reverie, I lead the horse over to his car. She shies at it and won't come close, so I hum to her and rub her forehead. "Steady now, sweetheart, you're fine, aren't you." And address Gus: "These girls are getting to be very polite, boss," I'd report. "They got manners, they got the good attitude too. Capernica here, she's very nice. You'll soon see if she's got the feet." Capernica plays monster with Gus, pretending he is one. Her part is to act all scared and tear around, showing off how quick she is. I should take her inside before she falls down, the idiot.

And Gus would say she looks fine, removing his cigar in appreciation. Which she does, in fact: a leggy bay yearling, healthy, filling out well and putting on some muscle. But mostly he'd want to see Dancer's Logic, one of his own horses, and a half-sister to Rotation. So we'd go into the barn and look at her in her boxstall, breathtakingly lithe and fine-boned. "This one knows her business, Gus. She's not a bad little horse, she might turn out." And Gus would be pleased, even at my understatement, already knowing what I'm telling him, but happy to hear it. We would stand there enthralled, the energy and promise radiating out of this young horse like daylight, her great bloodlines and her dizzying potential somehow part of the visible information. She embodies the mysteries of equine evolution, selective breeding, artful training and luck: she actually *is* the future of racing.

But switch off that happy memory: Gus is dead, and I'm looking at Logic by myself in the dim barn. In a couple of weeks, he would have moved her to his farm in Kentucky, and in the new year when she turns two years old, she'd start racing. I'd like somebody to tell me what I'm supposed to do with her now.

I tie her to a wall ring and brush her clean. Currycomb to dislodge mud, stiff dandy brush to flick off debris, soft body brush to put the hair back in place, and to clean her face and ankles. Glance at her teeth and gums. Comb the tangles out of her tail. Check her skin everywhere for scrapes or punctures. Feel her legs routinely for swelling or heat, pick around the frog of each hoof and look for soreness or softness that a bruise or infection could cause. Be sure that she has plenty of water. Refill her hay net in the corner of the stall. She moves around, watching me and puttering with her own thoughts, and I talk to her and sing and stroke her sleek skin. The air in the stable is fresh and light. I let her loose and serve up supper, a mixture of grains and a high-protein pellet supplement. The blend is balanced weekly, according to her weight and her growth chart.

When I get each of them in from the paddock, I do the same for the three broodmares, and for Capernica, and for Dave, who is restless from not enough riding lately, and for Sunny. I check the chickens and close up the barn.

If I had my way, I'd walk with Gus back to his car and say goodbye properly. I'd tell him how much I respected him, that he was the dad I hadn't had, and my mentor in racing. I'd hug him and tell him I'd miss him. I'd hold onto him and keep him from leaving.

Overhead, a chevron of geese is discussing the route south. Bird-watchers say the leader is neither dominant, nor more experienced, but usually a young, virile goose, who helps break the air for the others. The birds switch places as they tire, and use each other's low pressure air envelope to lift the flock. Long flight, group memory, smart geese. They sweep over, and their voices trail away.

I look around, at the big spruce singing, the solid barn, the fieldstone house, the fall air rolling up from the ravine and turning the two windmills. I've had enough loss. No more loss, please. Dad, Mom, Gus, that's enough.

* * *

I wake up afraid and recall the evening: we ate dinner, the kids went through their bath time routine, I read my book and fell asleep. I've popped awake, I've wakened myself with my own shout. The dream was so real, is it real? I listen to the house, eyes open in the dark, holding my breath. No, nothing...

The bedside clock reads just past midnight. I've been asleep only an hour. The dream was...my murder. The shadowy figure who killed Gus came for me. Afloat between waking and sleeping, this seems real. I am not safe, not safe, safety is a fool's illusion.

Frank has still not come home. Has he had an accident? Imagining a car wreck, I look out the window and see small snowflakes are silently falling.

He's not answering his cellphone. I slip down the hall and see that the kids are sleeping peacefully. Indy's getting better, breathing quietly. I go downstairs and pace in the kitchen for a while, and then pacing turns to tidying. The house is very clean, and I'm playing solitaire at the kitchen table when he finally comes in.

"Hey, Jeanie." He looks chalky, black smears under his eyes.

"Boy, are you okay?"

"Yes, fine, we finished up and wrapped this damn location. It was a little residential house crammed with delicate antique glassware. And the owner in there, wringing her hands, checking and rechecking all her precious stuff like she thought we were going to *try* to smash it if she turned her back. Why she didn't put it away when she rented her house to a film company, go figure. We're packed in there like sardines, by the end we're all ready to scream. Can you imagine? A room half the size of this kitchen, with fifteen people in it, and camera, lamps, cable, flags, stands and *attitudes*... Took forever. It was hot, it was slow, it was awful, and it's over, hurray."

"How does this china shop effect fit in with the gravel pit in this rock video?"

"The songwriter is describing his childhood."

"Oh. Do you want a beer, Frank?"

"Couldn't possibly. Maybe a sandwich?"

"Sure, there's some chicken."

We make the sandwich and sit on the couch while he tells me the stories of the day. Eventually, I stop feeling the aftermath of worry and start to have fun with him. I tell him about Indy's recovery, about speaking with the lawyer. I look over to notice that Frank has tipped over and fallen asleep, his empty plate neatly balanced on his hip. Remove the plate, cover the body with a blanket, climb the stair to sleep. When the roosters wake me and the kids, he replaces me in our bed.

* * *

"What's the matter with Dad?" Indy has passed him in the hall on her way down for breakfast.

"He was up late, honey. He's tired out from so much working these last few weeks. Are you hungry? Would you like Red River cereal?"

"Okay, with brown sugar on it and raisins."

"Of course."

"Me too," says Zazie, coming in, sitting down, then spreading her arms and laying her head down on the table.

"Rough night, Zaz?"

"I had a terrible dream. Indy! Move over! There was this guy, well, he was sort of dark and he had all this sticky-up hair..."

I don't always listen to these dreams, and today I'm still mulling over my own. I guess everyone is occupied by their dreams when first awake, but later in life, if we tell them, we get more concise. Zazie can hold forth for half an hour with no difficulty, her little voice going on and on, every detail. Always basically the same dream: entrapment, a scary antagonist, fear of the unknown. Growing up is awful.

I place the warm cereal in front of her and hug her shoulders. "Boy, Zazie, if I had a dream like that, I'd be scared. I'd want to wake up!"

"Me too!" She has a spoonful. "Do you have scary dreams, Mom?"

"Sometimes, but not often, not since I was a little girl. Maybe it's something you grow out of, when you've got a firmer grasp on what's real and what isn't." That ought to be true, anyway, right?

"I hope so," she says. "I'm growing out of it today."

"Good for you. Are you feeling better this morning, Indy?"

"A lot better. I slept all night. I'm just a little bit sick now."

"Atta girl. So, just take it easy today again, and maybe tomorrow you can go outside."

Upstairs, I can hear the shower running. Frank is up? He's had, what, five hours sleep? His gravel pit awaits. At least, it's stopped snowing.

When he appears, he looks pretty fresh. "This is supposed to be a short day, Jeanie, well, it has to be, it's daylight only. So we're starting as early as we can, and we should be done right after sunset."

"Okay, great. And you'll be at home tomorrow? I need you to stay with the kids, remember, while I go to Gus's funeral and to my meeting with the lawyer."

"Oh, that's tomorrow? Um, sure, I can be here. I was going to do some errands, but…"

"Jesus, Frank."

"No, I said okay, I'll be here. Take it easy."

"Good. Okay, have a great day."

"Thanks, you too." Tips his hat and slips out the door.

"I'm going to wake Lukie," I say to the girls. "He's got nursery school today. You ladies eat up."

* * *

It's a half-hour round trip to the nursery school so the girls have to come with us. They bundle up and bring books. They wait in the car as I deliver Luke to his playroom. Luke tears off his jacket and leaps in to greet his buddies. Three is a very sociable age.

Back home, I get Indy and Zaz set up at the kitchen table with their paints, sheets of paper, and lots of newspaper underneath. Fred Penner sings from the tape machine, and I'm back to work. I'm supposed to be training racehorses.

All summer, I had a low-key but regular schedule with the fillies. We've been through all that stuff about them letting me touch them, put saddles on their backs, and that they stand still once in a while. Three or four times a week, I've been taking them to the training track that we graded and fenced in the pasture between our house and the road. Last night's snow was light, and what's left is wisping across the hard ground, catching in frozen hoofprints in the barnyard. It's a little different terrain for young horses.

I brush Capernica quickly and tack her up. She's excited because she hasn't been out under saddle in four days. I make myself slow down to help her to relax. I mean to breeze her this morning, but when we get outside, I can see that's not going to happen. She shies at every little thing, the unfamiliar hardness of the ground itself spooks her. I let her walk and trot around the track twice before we even start to canter, but it's pretty hopeless. She needs more time to get used to winter.

I manage to fall off her only twice. The first time I land almost on my feet, keeping the reins in hand, and get back up on her. I take her around a few more times, collecting her firmly, packaging her strides.

Like all young animals, she is finding out about the world through trial and error, but at the same time she is having to learn a grown-up horse's business. She's doing quite well; she's acquired the knack of looking at the ground she runs over, so she doesn't fall down as often. She holds her head on a flexed neck, focussing her eyes and her attention on what she's doing. When she gets her legs untangled, she can move awfully fast, and she stretches and springs and revels in what she does best. Whoops, there's a flock of geese—that blows her concentration and down she goes. I hit the ground rolling and get away clear of the stumbling, somersaulting airhead. Back up, once more around and we can call it a day.

Capernica gallops nicely for one whole lap, and so I pull her in, turning around to walk clockwise for the stroll home. She walks around the track a lap, looking at things, cooling down, then we go back to the barn. I take off her tack, buckle a blanket on her and let her out in the paddock while I clean up her stall. I watch her rolling in the frostbitten grass as I call the kids on the barn intercom. Zazie tells me they're out of yellow. Run over to the house to mix up more yellow paint, but they've finished painting now. We read a couple of books together, cut up some apples for a snack, get out the big box of Brio train set pieces and get started building the track. When they're settled, I can carry on.

I bring Capernica inside, take the blanket off her, give her some hay, bolt the door to her stall, and then turn to Dancer's Logic. She gets the same lesson on the training track, then it's time to pick up Lukie.

# TEN

In the afternoon, we get more snow. It's dry and cold, and the wind blows it up in little twirls all over the barnyard.

The barn is warm, and I have the lights on. There's a certain song Logic likes to hear on the radio, a Shania Twain dance tune, and just now as it comes on I swear the filly starts swaying to the music. I lean on my pitchfork to watch her. Logic weaves and then startles, tosses her head and snorts when Lt. Det. Brock comes into the barn, banging the door and striding right over to where Luke and I are standing by Logic's stall.

"Mrs. Spring," he announces loudly.

"Hello there, detective."

"You are not one to waste time, I see."

"Well, I can tell that you like to perk right along, too. What are you talking about?"

"I have learned that you are riding these horses on your training track."

"That's my job, detective, yes."

"But you have no employer, Mrs. Spring, and no authority to train animals which do not belong to you."

"These horses need care and exercise. I would be irresponsible not to provide them with that."

"You are to desist from providing care and exercise to them. For Capernica, here, I have brought a court order on behalf of the owner, Arthur Connelly."

"Okay, good. This isn't Capernica, but I am happy to comply with any of Mr. Connelly's wishes concerning his horse."

The detective looks at me quietly, then shifts his eyes to Dancer's Logic, and back. "Where is Capernica?" he says.

"She's right in there," I say, indicating the next boxstall. Capernica swings her head out the dutch door helpfully. Brock is sullen.

"I certainly hope that you are correct, Mrs. Spring. This horse is to be transported immediately on the orders of its owner. I also have orders here to restrain you from contact with the following horses: Nevsky, Finesse, Fax Copy, and Dancer's Logic. Effective immediately, and until probate is settled."

"You mean I can't bring the broodmares in out of the snow, detective?"

He considers my question. "Transport has been ordered for these horses separately. I suppose you could bring them inside until then."

"Where are they going? And what do you mean about probate?"

"They are to be taken to the stables of the deceased, until the estate has been settled. As I'm sure you are aware, these horses belonged to Mr. Hampton, and in his will they are left to you."

"To me." I hadn't really caught that before.

"I see you are keeping your inheritance in racing condition." Condemning me from under bushy brows.

"And you would be less offended if I neglected these horses?"

"Offence is not the issue. You will await the settlement, and the animals will be tended by neutral parties."

Luke has been following the conversation, and he comes closer and takes my hand. I give him a squeeze and a wink. Actually, I'm glad to have less livestock to tend, and horse feed costs money. "Fine with me," I say. "I'm sure we'll all breathe easier with that arrangement."

"Hello?" Someone shouting from the barnyard.

"We're in here," I call, and walking to the door to meet the visitor, bump into Arthur Connelly, Capernica's owner. He enters the barn with another man, whom I take to be his stablehand or driver. Brock stands back silently.

"Jeanie." Arthur is stern. "I'm moving my horse. My lawyers have advised me to remove her from your care, in view of your legal status."

"Well, that's fine, Arthur, though, had you called first I could have had her ready for you. Are you planning to take her right away?"

"Paul brought his trailer," indicating Paul and the doorway. "Will you get started, please?"

Paul leans around Arthur and offers his hand. "Uh, hello. I could bandage her up if you show me where you keep her stuff."

"Okay, sure. The tack room is down there, last stall on the left. You'll find…" I realize that I'll have to show him where to find the big fluffy cotton rolls for Capernica's legs, and blue cotton bandages that hold them on. I go with him down the breezeway. "And her blanket is in there too, the blue Sydney Lake one is hers. Take any of those crash caps."

I come back to the owner. "Why is this happening so abruptly, Arthur? And what do you mean, my 'legal status'?"

"We just found out that you are a suspect in Gus's

murder. I can hardly allow our corporation to have any further dealings with you."

"I see. Excuse me, Arthur, I'll get your paperwork. Luke, please come with me." I'm contained.

"What's going on, Mom?" In the kitchen, Zazie looks up from her colouring.

"Mr. Connelly's here to pick up 'Pernica. And the police guy is back."

"Oh! Can I come out?"

"No, actually it's kind of ugly out there, sweetheart. Would you please stay in? And Luke, you stay here a little while too, just until the trailer leaves, okay?" I find Caperica's file folder in the desk in the office and go back out to the barn where Paul is suiting the horse up in her travel outfit. Connelly and Brock are standing back from the open stall door.

I hand the records over to the owner. "Here's her medical chart and my training notes, Arthur. I hope you have good luck with her, she's a good filly."

Connelly ignores my effort but takes the file.

"For God's sake, Arthur," I blurt, "I had nothing to do with Gus's death."

Paul leads the filly out of the stall and walks her out the barn door, her steel-shod hooves making a sharp, hollow sound on the rough cement floor. Arthur meets my eyes but follows without a word. You're very welcome, Arthur. I'll bill you.

"Detective Brock," I say, "do you know when the trailer is coming for the other horses?"

"Today, Mrs. Spring."

"Don't they have telephones? Gus's staff could have called me. And why did you come, anyway?"

"A courtesy call, really. I wanted you to know that you

are no longer under investigation for Gus Hampton's murder."

"What? And you let me go through that humiliating little episode just now? Thanks a lot. What poor bugger have you arrested?"

"I have no reason to tell you anything," he replies. "We have apprehended Mason Goddart. The murder weapon turns out to be his, and he confessed. We are confident we have the right person."

Luke and Zazie appear at the barn door. "Trailer's gone, Mom," she says.

"Thank you, my girl. Detective, I guess we've finished here, have we? Zazie, could you help me bring the mares back inside? They're going to be trucked out today too. Goodbye, Detective." The "fuck you" is only implied.

# ELEVEN

I call Hampton Farms on the barn extension, and the housekeeper puts me through to Joaquin.

*"Ola, chica, como estas?"* he says.

"Hi, Joaquin, whew! It's good to hear your voice. Are you doing okay, man? I got a little problem here that I know you'll have the answer for. "

"I'm okay, Jeanie. What's up?"

"I hear you guys are moving Gus's horses back to your place today."

"Yes, right. His lawyer is telling us this morning that we must move everybody back here. He phone you, eh?"

"No, he didn't, but that snake Brock was here to tell me. What a creep that guy is."

"I notice this about him too, yes."

"Well, that was my question, really. I hadn't heard a peep from you guys and then suddenly the police show up. When do you want to come for them?"

"I am sorry about that, Jeanie, yes. We are pretty busy here, it slip my mind to phone you. I can come get the horses whenever you like, *querida*, I could come now if you are not busy?"

"Okay, sure, I could have them ready in an hour."

"An hour is good. See you then, *mira*."

Zazie helps me catch the mares and bring them in from the paddock, and Luke runs around with the cotton tendon rolls. I give each of the horses a light brushing, buckle blankets and caps on them, and Zazie helps me wrap their legs in padded bandages.

Joaquin arrives with the six-horse trailer towing behind one of Gus's diesel fifth wheelers. He looks worn out, his large dark eyes bloodshot and shadowed. He's wearing a straw cowboy hat and pointed, heeled Texan boots, dirty jeans and not enough of a cable-knit sweater. He throws his arm around my shoulders as we walk back to the barn.

"All right, *mamita*?" with a soft grin drawn up into one cheek.

"I keep wanting to call up Gus and get his help with this."

"That is it, yes, Jeanie. He made life easy for us. He did the work."

"The police have arrested Mason Goddart. Brock says he confessed."

"I hear that too, yes. He confess after two days of questioning, they say."

"Really? That doesn't make him sound very guilty."

"Now I am not so sure, no. The knife was his, okay, but we have been using it at the track all summer to cut twine. It has been in the feed room all season. Plus Ned, oh, Ned is out of hospital, *querida*, he is on crutches, but his hip is going to be just fine... Ned says Goddart came to visit him at Etobicoke General on Sunday, which was the morning after the murder, and he was relax and normal, not like a killer, eh? Lukie! How are you, *hijo*? How is school?"

Luke comes bounding up and leaps into Joaquin's arms. "I go to school this morning, Walk-eem. It was GREAT. I go uuuuuup the see-ide, and doooooown, with the wind in my hair!"

"Oh, *que bravo.*"

Not like a killer, no, I'm thinking. Not the same as being somewhere else at the time, but pretty good. We all go into the barn where Zazie is in the stall with Fax Copy, patting her neck and saying goodbye. Faxy's due in six weeks, so she's quite round. We load the three pregnant mares into the trailer, and then Dancer's Logic. Logic loads well, up the ramp into the narrow stall, a little adult, off to her professional future. I don't know what will happen to her now. I assume Joaquin will take her with him to the farm in Kentucky when he goes, as she was scheduled to do. In a few months, she may move to Gulfstream track in Florida and do some racing. I don't care about that right now.

"Thanks for taking these horses off my hands, Joaquin. What is your status on the farm now? You still have a job?"

"I do until I have no more horses, *chica.* It's up to the owners to decide where they want their property to be. Otherwise, they keep paying fees and expenses to the accountant, and the accountant keeps paying me."

"So you'll take the racing horses with you to Louisville."

"Yes, Jeanie, an' the breeding stock will stay at Gus's farm until they are claimed."

"Joaquin, I've been wanting to ask you about something… Last Saturday morning, when I was talking with Gus, he suggested that I go to work in Kentucky, as an assistant trainer."

"I know, *mamita.* I help you get started at Churchill Downs, then I was going to replace Meryl in Florida for the winter season at Gulfstream. "

"And Meryl?"

"Was on his way out, *chica*. Gus was thinking over this plan."

"Did Meryl know?"

"Sure, he was in the face of Gus. Personal disagreements, I think so."

"Where was I for all this?"

"On the track, *querida*. You always riding."

"But we're all taking shipping orders from Meryl, he's running the horses now, as far as I can tell."

"It doesn't matter. It's good we can have somebody look after the business while everyone is so upset. We will settle with Meryl when the time comes."

It's getting dark and the wind is getting stronger. Joaquin bolts the loading doors of the van and hops into the cab of the truck.

"See you tomorrow, Joaquin," I wave at him. Logic bumps down the driveway, looking wall-eyed out her side window, trembling and brave. Goodbye, goodbye.

# TWELVE

"Are you still meeting with the lawyer this afternoon?" Frank's pouring coffee. The late morning snowstorm has stopped, the sky cleared, and the landscape outside is blinding.

"I called her last night after the dust settled, and she said we could postpone. She has nothing to defend me from. She said next time, she'll charge me."

"Next time you're suspected of murder? That's a relief, eh? Like knowing a good plumber."

"So, the funeral is at one p.m. I'll be back about three, I guess. You said you had some errands?"

"No, I'm good. They can wait. Take your time, Jeanie."

"Thanks, Frank. I appreciate that. Thanks for staying with Indy. I'll say hi to everybody for you."

"No problem, Jean."

The barn seems empty with only Sunny and Dave in there. I let them out in the paddock so I can shovel out their stalls. The two of them, the grey Arab and the black quarterhorse, have both had too much vacation. We've had no time to get them out under saddle in much too long. I finish up my chores quickly and go back to the house to clean up. Frank is giving the kids soup and sandwiches as I rush out the door.

* * *

Trinity Church is a beautiful old building around which the city has grown up, sheltering it now like a body around a heart. The temperature downtown is rising and the snow melting like springtime. I have parked my car for free on Shuter Street and walked the last few blocks on the slushy, sparkling sidewalks. Inside, the church is breathtaking, the stained-glass colours filling the steep arches of the ceiling, swelling up like the thundering music of the vast pipe organ. The front of the church is a riot of flowers, and the pews are packed with mourners. I find Joaquin and wedge in beside him.

Up in the choir loft, the singers are harmonizing "Jerusalem". I look around to see them and to scan the crowd. Trainers, track stewards, owners, jockeys, columnists and sports fans. Half of Toronto is here. Finally I spot Gus's ex-wife, Geraldine Hampton, way over in a corner, head bowed and miserable, sitting with Gus's only brother, Bing.

Rev. Stanley Templeton, who has been a benevolent and humane inspiration at this pulpit for close to a half century, climbs up to praise Gus. In his satiny red and ivory robes, he leads us. We are all bewildered by the violent death of a good man, and we try to focus on the useful life he led. Gus was a fair man who went out of his way to help his friends. He had his troubles, but he had grit and dignity. We will all remember him fondly and with respect.

Geraldine never raises her head, and Joaquin is weeping quietly, bent forward and lost in grief. It is Bing who gets up to deliver the eulogy. He's a corporate banker, a couple of years younger than Gus, taller and darker, resembling him more in manner than in appearance, for, like his brother, he manages to make us laugh. Bing shares some stories about growing up with Gus, who was as big-hearted and slapstick awkward as a kid, as he turned out to be as an adult. Bing reminds us of some of Gus's philanthropic moments, such as donating his end of the purse of his first stakes race win to kick-start a community safe house.

"I'm very confused to be here today," Bing is wrapping up. "This should never have happened, and it changes my understanding of what the rules are. Gus suffered, it was a cruel death, and he died alone. It can't get much worse than that. My only little ray of consolation is that in the last decade before his death, he was a happier man than he had been for most of his life, and that he was modestly proud of what he had achieved. He left the party before it was over. He would have been okay with that."

Bing Hampton steps down and returns to his seat beside Geraldine. She tips over against his sturdy arm and wipes her face with a tissue. Rev. Templeton comes back to tell us that Gus's body will be cremated, and that there is a reception up the street at the Sutton Place for family and friends. A single bagpipe circles up the octave, and people at the back of the church begin to leave. Joaquin holds my hand. No one is talking.

"Come on, buddy," I say. "Let's say hi to Geraldine and get out of here."

We find her. She's wearing black gloves, pearls and a big hat with a sweeping brim that she thought would make her look brave, but her face isn't holding up to her ambition. Their marriage naturally foundered when Gus came out of the closet, but their friendship was always on solid ground. Geraldine hugs Joaquin warmly and kisses his cheek. She turns to me and gives me a hug too. Bing stands back, hurting and unresolved, his eulogy like Geraldine's hat, all for show.

"Geraldine, will you allow…" I hardly know what to say to her. "I'd like to come see you, maybe next week?"

Her skin has an unearthly translucence, and her eyes are not quite focussing. "Yes, Jean," she answers quietly. "Won't you? Come next week, that will be wonderful."

We hug and part. It's agony, and I'm glad to get away.

I take the long way home.

# THIRTEEN

When I get home, I change back into jeans and check in with Frank. He agrees, so I go straight to the barn and to Sunny's stall.

"Hello, bub. Remember me?" He shakes his head and steps over. He has the classic Arabian conformation, overall a small, sturdy horse with big hair. The face is wide between the eyes, with tiny ears and muzzle, a deep chest, fine legs and hooves which, in his natural gaits, he lifts high and showy. I brush his dappled coat and put the saddle on his back, slip a hackamore over his nose and ears, swing open the boxstall door and lead him out of the barn. He stands still for the second it takes me to get on, then we step down the snowy path to the ravine.

I'm tormented by the need to solve this injustice. Really, who killed Gus? Whose terrible mistake was this? I"m not convinced it was this gambler, Mason Goddart. Two days of interrogation! He may be just a convenient answer, a wild card. Was the killer at the funeral today? Did I see him, shake his hand, as he pretended to mourn? Did he kiss the cheek of Gus's wife or grip Joaquin in a hug?

The afternoon is warm and dazzlingly clear, and Sunny is happy, snorting, playing, bucking in short hops. His hide is about the colour of the open water in the creek at the bottom of the valley.

He walks across it, rump deep, and canters along the other side until we reach the woods. Preoccupied, I'm not paying much attention to where we're going. There is a soothing quiet in here though, a few starlings yelling high up on trees where golden leaves still cling, snow-clad, and below, the creek running under hillocks of pristine snow. Roots cross the path, the horse has to dip his head to see them, arching his elegant neck and dancing light-footed. The trail widens into a roadway and clears under a canopy of birch branches. Sunny's bouncing all over the track, eager to stretch his legs. I secure my seat in the saddle and let him go.

Sunny springs away into an accelerating gallop, ears flat, tail up and streaming. He hits top stride in a few seconds, nimble charcoal legs below blurred in speed. The wind gets inside my cap and whips it off my head.

A rabbit is startled in our path. Sunny veers hard to avoid stepping on it, slips, and goes down heavily on his side, sliding off the road and thudding into the trees.

* * *

There he is, standing, blowing, head down, trembling, not far away. He moves around a few steps, limping a bit. I'd better get up and check his legs. Can't seem to stand. I'll just lie here a while longer. So dizzy.

* * *

Where's Sunny? Not over that way. Ahh, my head. Sunny, stand still. "Sunny, stand." That doesn't sound right. That's just a whimper. He won't understand that. "Sunny, stand." That's better. Atta boy. "Come over here a bit, would you?" Stop moaning like that, girl, you're scaring him, look.

"There, got you, good boy." Just sit a while. To clear my eyes, I wipe my face with some snow. It comes away red.
"You're pretty scratched up here, old fella. Any of these cuts deep?" I pull myself up on the stirrup strap, have a quick look. "Think you can give me a lift home, Sunny, my darling? We'll get you fixed up. Maybe Gus can come give me a ride to the clinic, might need a skull x-ray...
"Stand, now, whoa, so I can get on. There...you're so good...good boy." I lie on his neck, pat him. "Glad you know which way to go."
Sunny is throwing his weight into his shoulders to climb the steep hill from the ravine to the barnyard. At the top, I slide off him and navigate the barn door. He goes into his stall by himself, and I just let him. The barn phone is ringing. Must be Gus calling about the clinic. But before I can get to it, it stops.
There's a mirror on the medicine chest in the tackroom. It's me, all right. The face is swollen, is all, on that one side. I lean on the wall for a bit, then pick out the antiseptic and go back to have a look at Sunny's legs. His knees are swelling, and the hock and hip on the near side are scraped raw. But not serious. I clean him up and take my time getting the saddle off.

* * *

Frank is standing beside me, I'm sitting in the straw with the saddle across my lap. Frank lifts the saddle and helps me to my feet. Brings me out of Sunny's stall and closes the stall door.
"I see why you didn't answer the phone," he says.
"Was it Gus? I was going to call Gus."
"No, Jeanie. It wasn't."

And then I finally remember all about Gus.

Well, this is really something. Specific amnesia. A pathetic attempt to deal with the unacceptable. I sit down on a bale of hay.

"Geez, Frank. I'm pretty fucked-up here."

"Yes, my girl. Do you feel pukey?"

I do an inventory for concussion. Not nauseous. No more spinning. Focus is clear. "No, I'm okay, Frank. Just shaken up. And...I wanted to forget what happened to Gus, but now it's all clear as a bell."

"Did you black out? Should we go for an X-ray?"

I'm in a desensitized zone. I feel nothing. "No," I lie. "I'm fine. Let's go inside." But I don't move.

Frank stands quietly nearby, and in a while he sits down beside me and puts his arm around my shoulders. We sit, breathing. When I meet his eyes, I begin to cry. I lean my head on his chest and cry, and he lets me.

# FOURTEEN

No, actually, it's a wonderful idea," Frank repeats. "Of course, I don't expect you to notice that it's a wonderful idea. You're too busy throwing yourself off horses, sitting up all night worrying, and trying to solve crimes on behalf of the Toronto Police Department."

"Well, I've never been to Jamaica, so it isn't like, oh boy, that's just the thing we need, good old Jamaica."

"The kids will have a fantastic time. We need a break. You've got time before anything happens with Gus's probate, and you've had enough stress to satisfy any ten normal women. My wonderful movie, for which I have compromised the security of our home, doesn't begin until after Christmas. We could go for a week. Nothing can happen here in only a week. See? Great idea. A family vacation."

"I don't know, Frank."

"And YES, there'll be no—detectives!"

"Indy's still kind of sick."

"There'll be no detectives—today!"

"I love a Gershwin tune, how about you?"

"This isn't Gershwin."

"You know what I mean."

"Sure I do."

"Frank, I don't know how you do it, but I know that in no time at all you'll have me thinking you're right, we'd have a wonderful time and it would heal all ills to go sit in the sun. You glow with optimism."

"Perhaps, but you are quite brave for permitting yourself to trust my plan, even though it scares you."

"Actually, I'm very grateful for the way you stood by me a while ago in the barn. You didn't rush me, you didn't try to reason with me, you just let me feel rotten for a while, so that now I can feel better. That was very generous of you."

"I can be quite a sensitive guy when I need to be."

"You certainly can."

"MOM 'n DAD!!?"

"Yes, Lukie."

"Where a-a-a-are you?"

"We're in our room."

"You're in your bed! Are you having a NAP? It's not nap time!"

"No, we're just lying here."

"MOM! What happen to your FACE?"

"I fell off Sunny. Sunny tried not to step on a rabbit and he tripped, so we all fell down. But I feel fine now."

"Oh, okay. Can I get in bed with you?"

"Sure, there's a space right here."

"Want to pee-ay 'I Spy', Mom? I spy with my yitto eye..."

"I don't really want to, Lukie. I'm so happy lying here quietly."

"We can pee-ay so quiet-ye, Mom."

"Where are your sisters, Mr. Boy?"

"In their room, I think so, Dad."

"Okay, well, I want to ask them a question."

"Oh! I go get them for you."

"Thank you, Luke."

"Hey, Frank, telling the kids will be the same as deciding to go."

"I thought we did decide to go."

"Well, the idea was still in the sinking-in-phase for me. Why are you thinking about this, anyway? We don't have any money."

"No, actually, we have a bit. The movie needed a hundred twenty-five thousand, and I just slipped it onto the mortgage for one thirty."

"Thousand? Dollars?"

"How much worse does that make it? ...Jeanie? Okay, we could use that five thousand differently, you're right. We should, uh, set up an RESP, eh? For the twins."

"Just give me a minute, here, Frank."

"I was thinking we needed the time, Jean. The money doesn't matter. It's just a slightly more horrible miscalculation in my overall incredibly 'bad idea'. You know I'm good for it, honey, don't you?

"But, what matters is the state we're in. Look around, Jeanie. We need to get some time together, get ourselves sorted out. See this? We're having a little family crisis here."

"What is it, Daddy? Luke says you want to ask us something."

"A question about dinner, wasn't it, Frank?"

"Oh, yeah. I was thinking about a theme dinner tonight, girls. We can pretend we're going on a vacation, going someplace hot and sunny, flying there on an airplane, going somewhere where there are lots of flowers and big colourful birds, beaches and ocean and palm trees... Want to pretend that?"

"Sure, like a picnic dinner, Dad?"

"Yup, and we can fry some bananas for dessert, and wear our bathing suits, and eat in front of the fireplace."

"Okay!!!"

"Okay! So, let's get started. C'mon downstairs with me. What else will we have for our tropical picnic dinner?"

"Um, peppermints."

"Okay, Luke, we could have peppermints. What else?"

Their voices trail away, and I reflect on what a fantastic life I lead, and how much I love my dear husband.

# FIFTEEN

My contribution to dinner is to show up, in costume, and get the fire going in the fireplace. I then lie on the couch and listen to the activity in the kitchen.

"Zazie, since you're up on the counter, could you check for a can of coconut milk in the cupboard there?"

"Is this it, Dad?"

"Yeah, thanks. So, anyway, I was telling you about Jamaica. I went a few years ago, with Rosanne, when I was still married to her, and your half-sisters came too. They were about your age then, Lyra was eight, so Meg was six. They had a great time. Careful with that knife, there, Luke.

"I'm chopping this red pepper, Dad."

"You sure are."

"How much water do I put in the rice, Dad?"

"Are we baking this rice? We need two and a half cups rice, Indy, for all of us, with three and a half cups water. Luke, put your peppers in with the chicken, here, and Zazie, pour in that coconut milk. They use coconut a lot in Jamaica, coconut oil for frying vegetables. Not olive oil, they don't have olives. They have coconuts."

"On trees? Like on TV?"

"Exactly like on TV. Big coconut palm trees, bending over the white sandy beaches. The ocean is so blue! And salty! And the soft air smells of salt, and of flowers and growing things. So many colours, flowers and birds live there that we've only seen at the zoo. A billion stars in the sky at night and the ocean rumbling and strange shells washing up on the beach. Mangoes for breakfast, reggae music on the radio, sparkly little fishes in the water. You can go swimming with a diving mask to see them. The water is warm, all year long."

It's quiet in the kitchen, as the kids reflect.

"Now, do you guys want salad with dinner?"

* * *

Frank spreads a blanket on the rug in front of the fire and we sit in a half-circle, leaning up against the couch. There are indeed fried bananas for dessert, and with chocolate ice cream, they taste pretty incredible. I have finished the sinking-in-phase. Show me a woman who would not get on board with this fantasy.

"I was just wondering," I say. "If we actually went on a vacation to Jamaica, who would feed the chickens?"

Luke drops his spoon. "Or DAVE!" he wails. "Who would feed Sunny and Dave?"

"Well, this is just, 'what if', guys, so take it easy. Dave and Sunny could stay at Grampa Gus's farm with the broodmares and Logic. That part would be all right."

"And Marilyn, too, she needs dinner too," Indy points out. Marilyn is flat out on her side next to our picnic area, undisturbed.

Frank has another embellishment. "I was wondering how you might feel about Meg and Lyra coming with us, like, instead of visiting over Christmas. Rosanne would probably spring for their fare. I could ask her anyway. What would you think?"

"I love your girls, you know that," I say. "I think there's a lot to sort out for this family vacation."

Zazie whips her face around. "You mean we might really GO, Mom?"

"Well, yeah, but we have all these little problems to solve. Let's see how it goes, okay?"

"We might go *on an airpee-ane?*" Luke's astounded.

"Great idea, eh guys?" beams Frank. So while I'm doing the dishes, Frank and the kids get on the internet and look at hotels and air fares. Nobody books anything, but everybody knows where we're staying, when we're going and all about what Jamaica is like.

Then I get on the phone to Ned, who had figured to go to Kentucky with Joaquin, except now he's on crutches for six weeks and needs a place to live. He's staying at Gus's, but he's happy to oblige me and move here instead. So that works out perfectly. I don't even have to move the horses out.

The barriers to this plan are dwindling.

* * *

Thursday is a school day for all three kids. Indy's fully recovered and gets on the schoolbus with her sister at the end of our driveway. Frank drives off to do his errands, dropping Lukie at his nursery school at eight forty-five.

Ned drives over to have a look at the lay of the land. He's got his crutches under his armpits and is pulling himself out of his car when I catch up to him. Ned is about five foot six with pointed features, blue eyes and skin scarred by acne. An American, a bit of a cowboy, he's had some tough breaks, both of his bones and his luck, but hard work is his companion, and he doesn't complain. He's been riding for Gus for longer than I have, drawing pay, not purses.

"Thanks for taking this on, Ned. You're bailing us out here."

"Works for me, Jean," he says, settling his crutches comfortably, his weight on one foot. "I won't be gittin' on yer horses none, but I'll see they get outside every day."

"Lucky fools will have a vacation too."

"Yep. Well, y'gonna hafta show me all yer newfangled power sources, here. That solar panel stuff is Greek to me."

"Was to me too, but it's not at all mysterious. In fact, it's dead easy. Come around to the south side of the house, and I'll show you what we got.

"As far north as we are," I lecture, "and near the Great Lakes and so on, we only get an average of about four hours of insolation a day. Weather we been having lately, we haven't even used the solar boxes we got up there." Pointing at the black plastic equipment on the roof of the house. "Got black latex tubing up there exposed to the sunlight, water circulates through the tubing and is stored in the super-insulated hot water tank inside the house. Water temperature gets too low, it automatically stops circulating and the water heater coil flips on, powered by the grid. Cost us nothing to put the boxes up there, and it heats all the water we use in summer."

"Well, that *is* dead easy."

"The solar panels we have are on the shed roof, and you don't have to think about them at all. They have their own battery storage, and the power for the barn is produced by them. There's a back-up there too, there's never any problem."

Ned waves one crutch out toward the ravine. "Okay, so

what about them windmills?"

"They're little generators to produce electricity that we can use directly or store in a series of deep cycle twelve-volt batteries. These almost never fail us, since there's a breeze all day long up this cliff, or a gale more likely, but if the battery levels get low you can flip over to the grid. These turbines also pump water up from our well for the house and barn."

"S'pose you got yer septic out under that vegetable patch."

"Damn straight we do. You're on to that little trick too, eh?"

"My dad worked it that way back home. Okay, show me yer barn."

This tour has become an opportunity for me to appreciate what we have. As any farmer knows, the barn is the most important building on the property, and I'm proud of the fine condition of ours. I sweep along through the paddock, past the henhouse and into the stable, to show Ned the horses and feed room. We agree that dragging bales down from the hayloft is too much for his current handicap and designate a stall for storage while we are away. Ned visits with Dave and lets him out into the paddock. I check that Sunny's cuts are healing cleanly and lead him outside to stretch his bruised muscles.

Back in the house, we pour some cups of coffee, and I show Ned the cold storage cellar, the battery series, the pump room, the furnace and water heater. "Never gets near freezing down here. And unless we get a real cold spell, we mostly just heat the upper floors with the fireplace. The house is so thickly insulated that it's usually enough."

"This is a real efficient home you have here, Jeanie."

"Frank's fixed it so we don't have to tend it much, that's the nice part. He loves this stuff, the self-sufficiency and the economy. He's been so busy lately he hasn't had much chance, but you know he makes his own biodiesel out in the garage. Runs the tractor on used cooking oil that he's filtered and modified."

"A real go-getter, eh."

"Well, yeah, I thought it was crazy when he first told me about it, but I can't say it doesn't work. Diesel machinery runs all day for about five cents a litre and smells like french fries instead of soot. No monoxide, no sulphur, drive it around in the crops or in the barn, even, isn't going to hurt anybody."

* * *

When it's time to pick up Luke, Ned leaves too. "When do you suppose y'all'r leaving, Jean?" he says, squinting out his car window.

"I think it'll be Thursday, in fact, a week today, though we don't have confirmation yet from Frank's daughters. They were maybe going to meet us down there, we'll all vacation together."

"Quite a large group."

"Yeah, but they're great kids, I'm looking forward to it. They're about ten years older than our twins, so they get along really well. No rivalry."

"Well, I hope y'all have a real good time. Gimme a call when you want me to show up."

We shake on it. "Thanks, Ned. I'll call you as soon as we book our flight."

* * *

Friday while the kids are at school, I drive downtown. Gus's wife Geraldine lives in a condominium at the edge of the harbour that resembles a Caribbean cruise ship, sparkling white, tiered, and glinting with steel balconies and glass. I wave to the doorman, step into the elevator, emerge into a grand penthouse lobby, and tap at her door. Geraldine is wearing black and has been crying.

She serves me tea in a porcelain cup. She raises an eyebrow at my appearance. "Pardon me, Jeanie, your face is quite blue."

"I had a fall, Geraldine. I'm fine."

"Were I speaking with any other woman, I might be alarmed for you, and your husband. With you, however, I realize your story is probably true."

"You have had a terrible time, Geraldine. How are your bruises?"

"I just miss him. Gus was a dear friend."

"I know!" I puff my cheeks out, wincing. "He really loved you, Geraldine, he told me so about eight hundred times."

She doesn't respond, and we take a minute with our own thoughts. Mine, that I shouldn't be pressing this poor woman; hers, most likely, that I deserve her attention as Gus's protected employee. The view out the balcony window shows a very few sailing craft still moored in the cold harbour.

"Geraldine, I must ask you, were you aware of a change in Gus's behaviour over the last couple of weeks? I sensed that there was something really troubling him."

"He did seem agitated," she allows.

"When did you see him?"

Geraldine's delicate hair is honey-coloured and arranged softly around her face. She has a black silk scarf loosely draped around her reedy neck. She looks too thin. She begins, "Gus visited me last week, came to the apartment and told me..." She falters.

"This is wrong of me to ask. I'm so sorry, Geraldine. Don't say anything more, okay?"

For a while she composes herself, looking into her teacup quietly. She sets it down. "Jeanie, I think you and I have a similar...tenderness toward our late friend. I understand that you are trying to resolve the injustice of his death, and if what I know can help, then I shall tell you.

"When Gus was here, he asked how attached was I to the Swiss hotel of which he has, um, had...part-ownership. He needed to liquidate, access some capital, he said. Of course, it's his property, he can do what he wants to with it. So typical of Gus that he would ask me about that..."

She pauses and we sit. It's very quiet, high over the harbour.

In the smallest voice, I ask, "Did he say what the money was for?"

"Oh...Gus wouldn't tell, surely. Never for my ears. Never to burden me with the ugly financial details. He wouldn't take my help."

"Just, deliver, deliver? 'I'm fine, and here, do you need any money?'"

I'm a bit too blunt for Geraldine, though she acknowledges my meaning.

"He felt he had disappointed me enough. But racing wasn't quite the sport of kings, for him."

"You suspect there was something to hide."

"He was certainly a man who could live with a secret. But he would never have involved himself in anything illegal. You know that, Jeanie."

"Do you think he might have confided in Bing?" I ask.
"I've been wondering that too," she lifts her face. "Let me call and tell him you'll be coming by."

* * *

Over the next few days at home, we are in a perpetual state of packing. There is a lot of jumping on the beds, airborne clothing, drugstore visits for sunblock. Frank books low-rate mid-week tickets on the internet. He says he knows a great hotel in Negril, and they respond to his email to say "sure, slow week", they've got room for us.

* * *

Tuesday, I see Gus's brother Bing in his bank tower, in a richly carpeted and gorgeously furnished suite of corporate offices high over Bay Street. He's dressed for handball, shorts and a white T-shirt. He's agitated, however, and clearly in a rush.

"You look ready for some relaxing," I say hopefully, shaking his hand. "Good for you, Bing."

"My wife has insisted that we take some time off." He's gruff. "I can barely schedule it in, but we're going to the club together this afternoon." He gestures to a chair at his desk. "What did you want to see me about, Jean?"

I perch in the chair. "Thank you for making time for me, Bing. I know you have a heavy caseload, as well as your personal concerns. I was hoping you could help me to understand Gus's behaviour in his last week. I wondered if you knew anything that would explain, what seemed to me, unusual behaviour."

"Why are you asking me this?" He sits down behind

his desk as if I'm applying for disability insurance.

"Gus has been very kind to me, and we've worked together for many years. We've shared a lot of the excitement, and the worry, too, of his racing business. Lately he was very anxious, not like himself at all. I wondered if perhaps he had told you about it. Do you know what was troubling him?"

"Geraldine told me you had been to her place, doing some sleuthing. Does this investigation really concern you, Jeanie?"

"Certainly. The police have been to my home, and I have been interviewed twice. People I work with have been interrogated at length. Apart from my own anxiety, and my confusion about the circumstances of Gus's murder, I'm concerned about what was affecting Gus during these last few days. It's an unfinished conversation."

"You mean, the argument that you were having with him on Saturday." I think he's not going to say another word unless I am more forthcoming.

"Yes, okay. Here's what happened. He offered me a job as assistant trainer, to replace Meryl Connor."

"The guy that started work there last spring."

"Right. Except that over a month ago, I had already given notice to Gus that I wasn't going to be riding for him any more at all, that I had decided to spend more time with my family. A month goes by, he barely mentions it. Then, as if there had been some crisis, suddenly he's aggravated, frustrated by my lack of consideration for his pressures...which may have been justified. It occurred to me, though, that he must have been in extraordinary circumstances to suddenly need to manoeuvre me like that."

"And this came up out of the blue."

"Well, Geraldine says he spoke to her about money."

"She told me. Selling off the hotel."

"Doesn't that sound like he was in some sort of a jam?"

"Maybe he saw a better property. He liked to buy things."

"But you know him, Bing, he wasn't impulsive. You can't breed racehorses and want instant results for your efforts."

"Nor do you accumulate his kind of wealth without taking some risks, or occasionally acting quickly. No, Jeanie, I hadn't noticed Gus was acting strangely lately. We just saw him on the Labour Day weekend, and he seemed fine. I'm afraid I can't help you there."

My time with Gus's brother is slipping unproductively away. "You don't know of any difficulties he was having...trouble he was in? I know you did some financial work for him sometimes. Dammit, Bing, do you have any idea who did this to him?!"

"Sorry, Jeanie. As I've told you, on a personal level, he seemed okay. Since he was my client, confidentiality prevents me from telling you about business plans he was developing..."

I perk up at this suggestion.

He frowns. "Or might have been developing. I can only assure you that the police will find his killer, Jean. You should try to relax." Bing takes his own advice and his face smoothes. "Perhaps my wife is right, everyone should take some time off. Now I'm sorry to give you the bum's rush," he chuckles gently, standing, "but I really must get a few things quickly out of the way here."

Like me, I think. Get me out of the way. I don't feel Bing is being very candid with me. "Okay, thank you again, Bing. I know you're busy. Is it okay if I call you again, if I think of anything, or if you do?"

He corrects his face again, this time it's "concern". "You should just try and let it rest, Jeanie. We all have a lot of adjusting to do. We all miss Gus, and life is going to be difficult without him. Maybe you should let Geraldine have some grieving time too and not jostle her with your questions for a while."

* * *

Back home, Frank agrees. "He's a corporate banker, for gawdsake, Jean. He can't tell you anything, and even if he knew something or wanted to tell it, he would give his information to the police, don't you think? More the conventional approach?"

"It was the way he felt me out before he said anything at all, really. 'Why had I come to *him?*' 'Why was I asking?' 'How did it concern me?' Like he wanted to know what I knew, to know where he stood."

"You're pretty intimidating, you know, Jeanie. Especially with your face banged up like that. He probably thought his life was in danger."

"Yeah right, I might suddenly start tickling him or something."

"The Fickle Fingers of Fate!" Frank makes a leap in my direction, and I jump up evasively off the couch.

"I be the Ficko Fingers!" Luke cries joyously, digits aloft, Superman cape fluttering. "AAAAAA!!!" Sails onto his father, bedlam ensues. Sisters gleefully drop what they're doing to join the wriggling pile of tickling delight. I creep away to fester alone.

* * *

The night before we are to leave on our vacation, we do a final pack. Zazie is satisfied to take only her bathing suits and her Barbies. Indianna has planned carefully but has many, many sweaters. Luke has mostly sleepwear and stuffed animals, permitting the parent to detect the area of his anxiety. Frank wants to take all his bigger toys: scuba gear, the DVD player, an assortment of marine charts. I want five beach blankets and the patio umbrella. Eventually we get our load whittled down to what we can each carry, and everyone has a toothbrush.

Ned arrives as promised, and we do a last tour. He's brought a little backpack with his clean clothes and chooses the den to drop it in. He gives me an encouraging grin; I know the farm is in good hands.

# SIXTEEN

Can you go on a family vacation and be in your right mind? It's a great idea: everyone drops routine, leaves support and all that is dear behind, and crushes together, flung upon an adventure into the unknown. Since children want everything to be familiar, and parents hope everything will be exotic, how can this work? Yet people do it, they challenge the oxymoron, they attempt the impossible: they take family vacations.

The airport limousine arrives in the raw grey dawn. The kids are delighted in the big car, they whoop and run around the yard. Ned is up to see us off, game, hugging his coat around him in the wind. The driver loads our bags in the trunk, and we stretch out in the luxurious interior. We wave and wave, then lumber away down the driveway.

Frank spends the time riding to the airport preparing a list of things to phone back and talk over with Ned. I feel I've remembered everything and that Frank is showing a lack of confidence in my planning skills. I decide not to speak to him. He does, in fact, remember some fairly important details (like the location of the key to the house), which darkens my mood and gives an edge to his double-check routine. The girls find something to argue about too, and Lukie sings the same song over forty-three times, so by the time we reach the airport we all hate each other.

We find the longest ticket line of the five, and there we stand, anchored by luggage, wondering why we thought this would be fun. I concentrate on keeping the kids from getting lost. Indy and Zazie are at a comfortable age for travelling, though self-absorbed and not observant. Luke is not yet aware of travel. All of them could easily pass by a glacial avalanche in the Rocky Mountains without raising their eyes from their card game.

When we're finally checked in at the airport, we still have an hour or so before we can board the plane, so we wander around. Frank makes his phone call to Ned. There he is, nodding, gesturing, counting off items on his fingers. I join the queue to buy cups of orange juice for the kids, each at about the same cost as a light breakfast downtown. (Nice!) We stand in line at the duty free store. There's a lineup at the boarding gate, of course—this is the travelling game. It's a test of patience.

Other passengers seem as joyless as we. There are families sleeping together amid their luggage, exhausted upon the steel-armed couches. I think they were in line for something but gave up. There are caged pets here and there, packaged skis and surfboards, baggage held together with belts or plastic wrap or prayers. Some people seem in fact to have moved into the airport: black-shawled women knitting, schoolchildren studying, slick pimps preening. Other people are reuniting with their families, weeping, hugging. These ones have been released from waiting.

Finally we are boarded, and the plane is not a disappointment. We arrange ourselves diplomatically around the aircraft and don't fight about who gets the window. The kids love pre-flight candies and think flying is exactly as it should be. They put their chair backs up and down, up and down, choosy, seeking perfect comfort. After breakfast, they colour a while on their little tables. Luke is assembling an album.

"I drawing aw the seasons in this book," he tells Zazie. "Faw, winter, Hahyowe'en, Easter and Vacation. They aw in here."

After a while, the kids surprise us both by falling asleep. Frank and I have a drink and start feeling a bit excited and happy. We have a little time to focus on each other, to check in. We hang above the clouds. Pretty soon Indy and Luke wake up, and we visit the washrooms. They explore all of them, comparing supplies, washing their hands in each cubicle and enjoying the vacuum drains. Back in our places, I encourage them to experiment with their seat belts. On, off. On, off. Don't tell us we can't amuse ourselves.

Zazie wakes up and moves to a vacant window seat. The engines drone. We float between timezones, between lives. When we're set down in Montego Bay, we're ready for our new selves.

Find all the crayons on the floor. Repack the carry-on basket so everything will still fit. Stand in the aisle with everyone else, pressed silently against the strangers with whom, half an hour ago, we had exchanged travellers' intimacies. Door opens, and we're sprung into the clear sunshine and the wet, living air.

I'm instantly sweaty. My thick northern blood struggles with the weight of the humidity. The light is brilliant, the shadow at each person's foot has knife-edged perimeters. We follow the other passengers across the tarmac to the customs shed, over there with the sparkling palm trees, the bougainvillia vines, the hibiscus bushes, the casual gardenia shrubbery. Lukie touches the wheels of the airplane, squints up at the shivering silver fuselage. Come on, honey, smell this instead.

Of course, immigration takes forever. We stand and sweat. All the passengers are being processed at a single kiosk. After fifteen minutes, another customs official opens his booth. We race to form a new lineup. Twenty minutes later, another booth opens. We burst into action, dragging luggage and wilted children, to join those wishing to wait in the new area. We could choose up teams and have plenty of time for a good game of floor hockey. But this ambition is thwarted. Finally, we're through and ready to wait for Frank's teens to arrive from California.

We wander around the little airport. There are places to buy Jamaican souvenirs. Some very pretty silver jewellery, bright madras cotton, cute trinkets on keychains. Nothing actually made in Jamaica.

We buy drinks and lie on the thick crabgrass that is the terminal lawn. I think only crabgrass, or switchgrass, could grow in this sand and heat. A new approach, for me, to vegetation: moisture preserving succulents covering the hard ground, next to deep-rooted flowering bushes. Beach world.

The L.A. plane arrives a bit early. Same deal with the immigration guys, who rouse themselves from some other planet to perform their sanctified tasks. There's Lyra and Meg! Looking great, taller, elegant and lovely. Lyra now fifteen, as old as I was when I started working, poised, her backpack slung, jean jacket tied by the sleeves around her waist. Margaret at thirteen, with her dad's long black hair, is exotic and loose-limbed, shy and maybe a bit stressed from her transcontinental trip. We whoop and hop, they wave discreetey, hip level. They wait and wait, they go through, we shriek and hug. Now we're ready for our two hour bus ride to Negril.

* * *

The road winds west between the sea and an escarpment, this area completely inarable, but there are goats and donkeys grazing on tethers by the roadside. The bus whizzes fast around curves, past crazy green stuff, through the hot wind blowing off the water, past bending grass and wild flowers. Occasionally people get off, at hotels and villages along the way.

We stop for gas, and I go in to get something for the kids to drink. They've only got coke. In the tropical land of glorious juices, I hate to give them soft drinks. Water? There's a tap in the yard, she says. A tap? It's a free-standing spigot, in the oilsoaked gas pump area. I don't want to ask her if the water here is okay. I might offend her. She obviously thinks the water here is okay. For my little kids to drink? The busdriver finds a cup for me and fills it, and I hold it in my hands, looking into the warm liquid, hesitating.

"Oh, I guess I'll get cokes after all," I apologize. He snorts, impatient with the indecisive tourist. I've committed my first blunder. I look around. Frank's talking to some boys on bicycles. I drink the water and return the cup to the proprietress when I buy the coke.

* * *

Negril is a small town, a sort of end of the world place to which travellers struggle and may never leave, like Key West and Las Vegas. Those attracted here could hardly vary more. There's a hippie community at least four decades old, and beside it, boomers perk themselves up in an all-inclusive clothes-optional resort. The biggest reggae stars appear in midnight beach concerts, as pseudo-Rastas burn through town on their Harley Davidsons. Here and there are ferocious vendors up from Kingston, peddling silver jewelry or knives, giving new meaning to aggressive salesmanship. And everywhere there are sunburned tourists staggering around trying to score, or cross-eyed having scored the mushrooms or the grass or the 140-proof. No wonder the locals are sometimes cranky; they have a lot to put up with.

On one side of town is a seven-mile white beach, dotted with resorts and bars like floats on a fishnet. On the other, hotels are built into and atop a cliff jutting twenty feet out of the multi-coloured, crystal water, peaceful as a pond. This is where we're staying.

The bus drops us at a place called Home Sweet Home, a hotel enclosed by a nine-foot fence and patrolled by a doberman. She lifts her head off her paws for a second when we walk in, then returns to her doze. Frank tells me she's trained to harass only black people.

Each room of the hotel is a separate building, in which the roof is the principal feature. We approach the common room, a round low-walled grass-thatched hut, arranged like a cafe, with two long tables set in the front half and a kitchen filling the back. Sitting together, their feet propped on the knee-high wall, the innkeeper and the cook are drinking bottles of Red Stripe.

"Help you?" The owner is deeply tanned, a dark-haired American woman in madras shorts.

"Hi, we emailed you this week? We'd need, oh, two or three rooms."

"Oh yeah, I answered your letter, I'm Eve," says the American. "Ruth? Where are we putting these people?"

Ruth is a fed-up local resident. With some disdain, but with a little warmth for the children, she shows us our rooms. The teens get ground-level accommodation near the sea cliff. For us, a circular grass-thatched treefort nested in a huge banyan tree in the middle of the property. We climb a stairway from the base of the tree, through a trapdoor into a regular-looking hotel room with a large glassless window on the ocean side. There are two double beds, and Ruth is wrestling up the stairs with a cot for Luke. Each bed has a mosquito net knotted gracefully above. The girls choose their bed, and we drop our luggage at last.

"First, I want a shower, no, a swim," says Frank. "Want to see the ocean, kids?" Of course everyone wants to see the ocean, so we dig through the suitcases for a change of clothes.

"No, that's *my* bathing suit," wails Indy.

"Is *not!*" snaps Zazie, who has had entirely enough co-operation for one day. Indy sobs, all her travel fatigue and tension triggered by this good excuse. Luke feels it's time for a game of cards.

"Will you pee-ay with me now, Mom?"

Right. You don't just go swimming. So we clean up business, and the bathing suit pretext gets solved, and eventually we have our suits on and go out through the trapdoor, around the roots of the tree, join up with the teens and move on to the cliff edge. There are stairs down to the water built into the rock, but no beach at all, no shallow water either. I stand agape.

We didn't bring life preservers. The girls swim quite well, for six years old, but not *this* well. And Luke, hey, he's pretty little. Aaggh. No lifeguard, no sleeping under your book on the deckchair. "Wait a second, Frank," I say. "We'll have to watch the kids every minute that they don't drown."

"It'll be okay," says Mr. Optimism. "Look here, there's a sandspit on the left. Anyway, they're old enough to be careful. Furthermore," his ace in the hole, "we have two lifeguards right here."

Meg and Lyra flash small smiles. Okay, oceans are not uncommon to everyone. Hmm. But why didn't we get a place on the beach?

The kids are playing cave, hiding, exploring the ledges and crannies in the cliff-face and moving acrobatically among the rocks, along the broad pathways up and down, without accident. Maybe there's more to life than swimming.

Frank dives into twelve feet of water at the rocky edge. There's a curve to this hotel waterfront: an edge that falls almost vertically, like off a dock, and nearby a gradual slope of sand that's built up against a jumble of rocks, the "sandbar", sticking out into the bay. The big girls get right in, clean dives straight into the water. I fall into the ocean in my turn, opening my eyes to see the white bottom, a few butterfly-coloured fishes zipping by, and a lace of caves in the cliff below the surface. The salt water is very buoyant. I pop up to the top and see Frank and the kids watching me, and I want to hug everybody.

Frank holds Indy's hand at the edge of the sandspit. She steps on, and I come over to navigate Zazie. Luke stops his cave exploration and wets his feet. We wiggle our toes on the sandy bottom and dunk ourselves in the warm still water. Meg and Lyra are sunning. There's no wind, just the soft, tired air and the slow swish of ocean. We sit down, the kids immersed up to their armpits, us to our ribs. There we are, the Canadian family, white as paper, gazing out to sea.

* * *

The shower's an outside job, semi-enclosed by fieldstone, overgrown with vines, open to the sky. We all hose off the salt and walk up to our fort to change. Frank wants to take us to a certain restaurant for a sunset supper. He calls a taxi from the phone in the common room, where the two other hotel occupants are sharing supper with Ruth, and the owner, Eve. It seems if we buy food, Ruth will cook it, and we can share the budget with the rest of the tiny hotel. The other people are Virginians, young lovers, very brown from three weeks in this sun. They are slow-moving fun-seekers, Bobby and Adele. Bobby offers us a beer.

We sit with them and await the taxi. Ruth has fried their chicken in coconut oil with some chilis—it smells pretty fantastic. They're also having coconut oil-fried chips, calaloo mixed with onions and allspice and avocados sliced with mangoes and limes. Frank and Bobby are talking about windsurfing.

Eve says she's had a wire from New York, she's thinking about leaving tomorrow to visit her sick uncle. She asks where we're going for dinner, and when Frank says Rick's Cafe, she asks if she could share the taxi with us.

She lives in a loft over the kitchen. She comes down the ladder wearing white linen pants and shirt and a broadbrimmed hat she tilts down over her cheek. The teens and the taxi arrive together and we drive up the coast road, away from town. We circumnavigate reeling tourists and fiery revolutionaries. The restaurant is on a jet of land, stuck out over the ocean, a clear view west and south, with the sun touching the horizon as we find a table at the patio's walled edge. Eve orders a banana daiquiri, and shades her face against the coral sunset with her hat brim. Frank observes her quietly.

Service is slow, but we are good at waiting, we've had practice. There are hawks circling over the water. As the sun sinks, the spectrum lies horizontally on the edge of the world, like a straight rainbow, every colour reflected in the sea. The soft night wind smells of orange blossoms. Eve meets her friends at the bar and sits with them.

We have snapper in saffron sauce, sliced potatoes and beans with coriander. The little kids don't like the food, but they're happy playing with the tiny lizards in the sand under the table, and that's fine for the first day. Meg and Lyra need boy repellant in a big way, chaperone-ship won't be no piece o' cake.

Frank and I hold hands, another check-in. We may survive this vacation. If nobody drowns or gets sick, if the little kids meet other kids to play with, and if the big kids don't meet too many. Offspring take up lots of space, and that's the deal.

We walk home, Luke piggy-back, the others bumping and shuffling. Tarantula scuttle in the whitedust evening road, and frogs sing in the trees.

Frank sits with his daughters in their room for a while. I lay the little ones under their mosquito nets and pull two chairs over to the window to watch the night. The kerosene lamp swings gently in the ocean air. Frank comes in, and we sit.

We will all get what we want. For the kids, we will stay the same. For ourselves, we will do the same things exotically.

When we fall into our bed, there is no waiting for sleep.

# SEVENTEEN

I wake up, sit up, look through the mosquito net and across the room, out the open window, to the twinkling sea. Green lush growing things, birds, flowers! Incredible!

Climb out from under the net, past sleeping kids, and creep down the stair. Roosters are hollering down the road. There are canaries in the trees. Backlit by the dazzling new sun, a lizard blows up his ruby throat. Early light on the sparkling jungle, papayas growing like smooth green breasts, scarlet hibiscus flowers high on a twenty foot tree: this is paradise. Here, a hummingbird hangs over a bloom three times his size, his wings invisible in their speed, his little emerald body brisk in the sharp light. My hands are wet with the humidity, my hair has frizzed overnight. Ruth arrives, and I have some of her coffee.

She has a way of treating me as if I were a child that I don't find too hard to live with. I'm from another world. There's a lot that I've never seen before that she takes for granted. I'm happy to have someone I can ask dopey questions.

She's telling me about the market at Savannah-la-Mar, the next town, when Frank and the little ones come in for breakfast. Ruth likes the kids just fine. Her face lights up and she slices mangoes for them and hands around bowls of yogourt. Frank asks about Eve, and Ruth says she has left already for the airport. She'll be gone two weeks or more.

The kids play in the plants outside the common room hut. Eventually the teens show up, drink coffee, tell us what they dreamed about, apply sunscreen and comb their beautiful hair. The sun moves along, and the wind comes up a bit. Gradually, we decide to visit the beach.

The tar road is already bubbly as we set out. Zazie and Indy hum to themselves and watch their flip-flops. Luke is skipping, Frank carries the beach blanket, I've got the towels. Meggy and Lyra enjoy the attention of hordes of young men. When we find a place on the sand, the kids dig in right away, shovelling, building, poking along the waterline for shells to decorate their castles.

Frank stays with them, helps them discover the water, holds their hands in the soft swell. He's taking great pleasure in showing them this world. He finds a swim fin in the shallow water and brings it ashore. Astonishingly, after a moment, a tiny octopus, shiny black, climbs out and scuttles for the water. We are startled and amazed. How well he runs! And how does he know which way to go? Meg and Zazie replace the swimfin in the sea and search the water, hoping to recover a pet.

Canada is a million miles away. The horses, the cold, poor Gus's murder and his mystery are a movie I attended. This is real life here. Lyra is stretched out, reading, on the blanket next to me. She sets down her book and turns on her side.

"Dad looks happy, Jeanie," she says.

"Doesn't he? In his element. You see him last night at dinner, talking with that Rasta guy about wind turbines?"

Lyra snorts. "You can take a man out of the country..."

"But you can't get that guy to lay down his tools for anything, right?"

"Drove Mom completely nuts. She's a Hilton Hotel kind of girl, you know?"

"You guys moved out of that suite though, what, last August sometime?"

"Yeah, we're in a house in the Hills now. It's okay."

"And she's doing well?"

"She's good, yeah. New boyfriend, a director."

"Yikes, what's *that* like?"

"He's nice. She's happy."

"Wow, aren't you all adjusted!"

Lyra elbows me and giggles. Indy comes up with a shell collection and the moment passes.

We all get really hot. On the walk back home we stop at a stand for some curried patties and eat them as we sweat uphill to Home Sweet Home. The ackee pattie is fantastic, a rich yellow bonanza. This afternoon I have to get something for our communal dinner. I've seen a guy trucking lobsters around in a pick-up, I'm hoping to catch him later.

Siesta. Drift away, the turquoise framed by eyelashes. Wakened by a noisy afternoon rain, I stand by the window to see it pass out over the ocean: a grey curtain, beaten water. A rainbow comes out, so close, one foot in the sea and one in the forest, a complete arc, a perfect half circle, its ghostly colours dissolving into the bluegreen waves. I can see through it, bizarre, like looking through time.

I go outside and sit in the arms of the tree roots. There's a strong sailing wind blowing chop on the water.

I'm tired. Blood's moving slowly, eyes drooping, I'm acclimatizing. Flesh tingling from this morning's beach trip. I'm unfamiliar to myself. This languor, I'm a sensual zombie. I can't think.

Heavy leaves around me sway and drip. I drag myself over to the gate and am immediately confronted by salespeople. Two women are passing, each with coolers balanced on their heads. They seize the opportunity, seize me.

"Here, motha, you need some 'o dis nice fresh juice. Looka dis."

Yup, the coolers come off the heads, there's ice in there, there's coke bottles filled with beautiful fruit juice and corked. Amazing. "Sure, yeah, I'll take some, I got lots of thirsty kids."

"Oh, den you betta have somma dis sowasop juice too, motha. Children like dat so much. How many children you have?"

I explain our entire situation. They each have plenty of advice for me. I pay them and reel back inside the nine-foot gate. They were nice, and we need the juice, but I can't get used to how personal everyone is. You can't ignore anyone, like city people do. If you're in sight, you must be up for some action, some transaction, some conversation at least.

* * *

When everyone wakes up, we loll around awhile on the rocky ledges. We notice the Virginian couple sunbathing without clothes on a shale platform about halfway down to the water. The little guys think this is marvellous and immediately take off their bathing suits. The big guys think it's gross and immediately return to their room. After a few minutes in the sun, we're all suffering from the heat, and we stagger over to the common room hut for juice.

"We gotta go shopping, Frank, replace what we've eatten, get some dinner. Want to walk up to that bar where we saw the lobsters yesterday?"

"Okay, sure." Frank is pink, and his eyes slightly crossed. He suffers quietly.

"I'll come with you guys," says Lyra.

"Not me momma, I stay here." Luke is developing a relationship with the doberman. She's a nice dog with a huge tick on her back. I saw Ruthie spraying it with Raid.

"Not me either, Mom. I want to swim!" Our sportive Zazie.

Meggy flings her hand over her head from her deckchair at the cliffedge. She's got her book, hat, sunglasses: she's staying.

"Not me, I'm tired of walking." Indy looks like I feel.

"Hmm. Could you stay with them, Frank? Especially if Zazie's swimming..."

Frank is glad to stay, so Lyra and I step out the gate. The road is fiery though the day is well along. The bar is a twenty-minute walk, past fenced motels, overhanging flowering trees, a pattie stand and a corner grocery. There's the usual thick traffic of dazed tourists and exasperated Jamaicans. Lyra causes a stir as always but glides along beside me unperturbed.

"Do you remember much about your trip here before, Lear?"

"Not a lot, I was pretty small. And we were in a different town, for sure. I remember the beach, and the water was wild, not this protected cove. We stayed in a big hotel."

"More your mom's speed."

"Yeah, she's a little bit stuffy that way. I like this town." We have a small parade of young men following us, chatting, rough-housing. "I remember one day there was a storm, the waves were *huge*, and the noise just deafening. And there were kids out there, playing in the surf, you could just barely hear their little voices above the smash of water. Made a big impression on me. I was afraid for them."

"You are a very compassionate person, Lyra. Always have been, since I've known you."

"Oh," she says, deflecting the compliment, "I just hoped they'd be okay."

A pickup is parked in the shade at the entrance to this cliff-edge bar. Lobsters are half-submerged in melting ice water, a bit dreamy but still defending their spaces with slowing waving claws. They're gigantic, each of them two or more feet long.

"Will you be here awhile?" I ask the driver. "We want to get a drink and then take some of these guys home."

"Dat is cool, motha, but soon come."

"Okay." We head for the thatch-roofed bar. A few people are sitting on the stools in the breezy shade, sipping things out of coconuts. Some are sitting on deckchairs in the full sun, playing backgammon and chess. The few Jamaican guys here are hustling girls or talking earnestly together in groups. At the edge of the patio, a stairway leads down to a snorkelling rental shack. There are swimmers tooting through the perfect water, spearfishing.

We order papaya smoothies and sit in the shade of a big palm. Lyra stretches her long legs out and leans back in her chair.

"Okay, where were we... Your mom's new friend is nice, so that's great. And how's school?"

"Well, I'm liking it better this year. My second year at this high school, you know, I know where everything is and which clubs are for me, and all that. My teachers are mostly just great this year, like, I didn't get the History Horror that everyone was afraid of, and the visual arts teacher is *just... way... cool.*"

"That's for photography?"

"Yeah, and we're developing our own pictures now and going on field trips. It's really fun."

"You bring your camera with you here?"

"Of course! But I forgot to bring it just now." She looks around. "There are some great-looking faces here."

I look around too. There are some men standing together near the cliff edge, three Rasta guys with faded T-shirts and mirror sunglasses, and an Italian, black hair curling down his shoulders like a lion's mane, a long moustache on his dark face, a real brooder. He feels me studying him and stares back with green steady eyes. I feel myself blushing.

"You take pictures of strangers, Lyra? Isn't that, um..."

"Provocative? Well, I don't like walk up to them and snap, Jean. I try to be discreet."

"Oh, like a sleuth, a P.I. Wow, I haven't told you all about the mess at home, honey, this is a huge story. My dear buddy Gus was murdered." I lean in and fill her in on what little I know about the incident. I decide not to tell her that I was suspected in the case, because it's just bullshit and would only make her feel worse. I do describe how her dad had just finished a string of tough projects.

"So that was it, we needed this vacation. Your dad and I

were both completely stressed out and ready for a break. It's so cool that your mom let you girls come with us."

"Yup, she likes you, you know. She thinks it's okay for us to spend time with you, and of course we get along great with Dad. And since our school is semestered? Exams are six weeks away, no pressure. But Jeanie, wow, you've been with Gus forever. This would be so hard on you."

"Thanks, sweetheart. It's grisly. I miss him so much. Times like these, it seems there's no sense to the world... Wait a second! Look where we are! Really, it does me so much good to see you girls. You look so well, and you're both such solid, good kids."

Her composure unrattled, Lyra grins at me and toasts me with the last of her smoothie. "Yeah, Meggie's doing fine, she's at a new school..."

Lyra fills me in on the family news. The air moves around, the sun starts to sink, and we rest in comfort.

* * *

When we get up, we go to the pickup truck to select five monsters for dinner. On the way home we stop at the roadside grocery and pick up some oil, beers and potatoes. The saleswoman looks at me doubtfully.

"Yer not going to put dis oil on yer skin, are ye? De coconut oil is very dear in Jamaica."

No, ma'am, we're going to cook with the oil. She lets me purchase a litre in a recycled wine bottle, and seeing the lobsters twisting in my burlap bag, gives me some limes to squeeze.

Ruth thinks I've been conned, to pay so much for the seafood. She clicks her tongue and mutters about tourists and their stupidity. I had thought I was getting the deal of the century. Ruth splits the lobsters and broils them with a baste of coconut oil and grated ginger. The potatoes are sliced and fried. Bobby and Adele contribute a salad. We drink beer and watch the end of the sunset.

The whole sky moves by and the moon gets brighter, and we can see rain coming across the grey water, looking like the sea leaping up into the clouds. We sit with our feet up, listening, watching as the storm passes over. Stars shine afterwards and a zillion crickets sing in the bougainvillia bushes. Somewhere down the road, the usual radio reggae is being drowned out by a live concert. One of the bars has a band in tonight. The one-three rhythm lifts through the heavy air, and the little ones sway on their chairs. They brush their teeth at the outdoor sink and amble up to bed. I go to settle them in.

Indy and Zazie have laid their pillows down the centre of their bed, I guess to mark their territories, but they are both cuddled on one side together.

"You guys look so cosy there."

"Zazie asked to sleep on my side tonight," reveals Indy.

"Zazie, why do you want to sleep *with* Indy, when she's so close already?"

"Zazie likes it when I hug her, then she's not afraid," says Indy.

"Of the dark, you mean?"

"Yeah."

"So why aren't *you* afraid?"

"Well, I'm older."

"Indy, you're two minutes older."

"Yeah."

Luke is face down on his cot, out like a light. I lie down with my girls, talking about how maybe tomorrow we'll take the bus to the market at Savannah-la-Mar, see what they've got. They're pleased at the idea of an excursion. We look out the window at the stars awhile, and I hear the girls drift away. I tuck in their mosquito net and go back out into the velvety night.

* * *

Frank meets me at the foot of the steps, and we walk to the cliff edge, listening to the dark, the water, the reggae.

"Wanna dance?" Frank puts his arms around me and leads a slowstep. The moon is so bright, we cast sharp shadows on the rocks. As the band next door winds down their song, Frank is a hot ghost in my hands. He kisses my mouth and touches me, whispering. He's like someone coming up out of water, slowly surfacing, moving into focus.

Frank cups his hands over my buttocks, gently rocking me against his hips. He's shirtless, feverish with sunburn, tingling with gooseflesh in the soft air. His whole body is sensitized, vulnerable. He smoothes his hands up my back, lifting my shirt. His chest hairs brushing my skin make me shiver. He moves slowly, a dreamwalker, his senses sparking in his fingertips.

Meggy has come out to find us, and when she does, she's embarrassed. At thirteen, everything is deeply embarrassing.

"Oh, hi, sweetheart. You taking a stroll?" Frank's hands drop to his sides, my shirt falls into place, we smile stiffly.

"Dad, oh, God, I'm so sorry." Meg attempts to climb underground.

"Not at all, it's okay, honey. You're allowed to walk

around!" I touch her arm. "It's just so darned romantic out here... Frank, we need to be more furtive!"

Meg laughs. "Adults sneaking through the bushes..."

"Absolutely no overt necking!" adds Frank. So we make the best of it and go back to the common room hut together.

Adele and Bobby are sitting side by side at the table, sharing a cigarette. They talk quietly, touching often, absorbed with one another. They almost breathe each other, they're so attentive to their chemistry. They turn to welcome us, their hands still talking in a private hum. No wonder Meggy left them alone.

"Where's Lyra?" I say.

"Just left a second ago," says Bobby. "Went to see the band down the way."

"By herself?" I run for the gate. She's about fifty meters out, swinging along down the road.

"Lyra, wait a sec!" She hears me and turns around. I jog down to meet her. "Honey, I don't think you should go off by yourself without telling us where, especially not at night, you know? Let's go back and just talk this over a bit."

"Oh, Jean, it's cool, I just want to check out the band. I told Bobby..."

"Okay, yeah, but not by yourself, eh? We could go too?" I dunno. How old do you have to be to go off alone at night in a resort town? Damn, I should have thought about this.

Meg and Frank catch up to us. "What do you think, Frank. We go with her?"

"Yeah, hell, I'd love to see 'em. Meggy wants to come too."

"Okay, hmm, I'll see if Bobby and Adele can keep an ear out for the little guys."

"They were going out too, Jean. They're just getting their stuff together now."

"Oh, bummer. Well, I'll stay. You guys give me a full report."

"Aw, Jeanie..."

"No, it's okay. I'm tired anyway. See you later." I do feel tired, heavy and sluggish. I don't mind.

"Okay then, see you!" The girls might be happy to have their dad to themselves anyway. Off they go. I meet Adele and Bobby as they come out the gate, and we exchange a news update. Now everyone knows where everyone is—we're very organized.

Zaz and Indy are sprawled all over their bed, like swimmers exploring. Insects whine and sizzle outside my mosquito net, a creature scratches in the grass roof. Lukie snores lightly from his draped cot. I lie down and watch the night for about ten seconds...

# EIGHTEEN

It's mor-ning!" Zazie, backlit by the brilliant day, is sitting alertly inside her net. Indy wakes, drags herself upright and gazes blankly out the window. I feel stiff. Frank's side of the bed is undisturbed.

We dress and shuffle around our room. I'm singing part of a soulful song I like, getting myself going. "Tell me some-thing good..." After a while I sing the line again.

On the third repeat, Zazie uses the same tune to substitute her own line: "Those are all the words I know..."

"Hey, you know that song too?" I hug her, she laughs.

Lukie sings, "Tey-o me sum-ping good..."

My god, we're the Partridge Family.

"Is anyone hungry? Off we go! Breakfast!"

* * *

Ruth is sitting in the common room hut, drinking coffee with another woman. She says she has chores to do, and as she leaves she introduces us to her sister, Anicea Dunbar. The younger woman is a freedom fighter of the willowy kind, with a smooth, calm face and quick eyes. She is wearing a long loose dress and an elaborately tied scarf to hold up her dreadlocks. Her two babies are with her, about three and five years old. Sweet kids, very low-key, round, playful fellas. I like their mom before she's spoken.

"Happy to meet you, Jeanie," she says, offering her hand and her acceptance. We shake, and the kids mingle. I move over to the propane stovetop and finger a frypan. Humm. Eggs in the fridge, bananas on the counter, Frank nowhere at all.

Ruth comes in from raking footpaths, and I tell her to sit and let me make her some breakfast. She's fairly sure I'll break something but joins Anicea and plays with her nephews at the table. I fry some slivers of Spanish onion in coconut oil, sprinkle in some cumin seed and black pepper, then chunks of banana. Beat eggs and slide them into the pan with everything else. Ruth has baked a cornbread that is cool enough to cut. We finish off the orange juice. Everyone thinks the eggs are pretty good. I think maybe the two Jamaican women enjoy letting someone else do some cooking for a change.

I walk down the path to Meg and Lyra's hut and peer inside the shuttered windows. Dim interior, twin beds, twin mosquito nets, two girls sleeping soundly in their beds. Okay.

I put in some time back at the table, waiting to see if he'll show up.

Anicea is a poised and graceful person, with great tenderness for her boys. As we are talking, I realize I've met a woman like her before. My own mother was also a single mom, living a thoughtful and self-determined life, taking hard work without comment, strongly feminist and very gentle. It emerges that Anicea is a farmer, supporting herself by supplying local markets with goat cheeses. I want to sit and mooch off her energy for a week or two. Now there's a vacation.

But I'm preoccupied and not good company. Our talk moves around to my idea of a bus trip to Sav-la-Mar. Ruthie gives me directions, which bus, how long, when to get off, how much. I'm all set.

"Ruth, I believe our big girls were up late last night."

"Yes, motha."

"Well, I want to go on this shopping adventure, but I don't want to wait for them to wake up. Can you give them a message for me?"

"I can do dat."

"Good, thanks. Is there anything that you need that I could get for you at the market?"

"Dey have a spice store dere, alotta variety. You could get me some a dat. De stores here have just a few tings."

"Okay. Would it be reasonable to think we'd be back by mid-afternoon?"

"Yes, Jeanie, it is. About an hour dere, or less. I tell your Frank."

She's just looking at me, straight and flat. Husbands run off all the time, no problem. Okay, fine. I say, "Thank you Ruth. Anicea, very good to meet you. I hope you bring your boys by again soon. These kids get along okay together, eh?"

Parents do that all the time, line up playmates. Anicea doesn't mind. She smiles and says we'll see each other again.

We collect our hats and footwear and go out to the road to catch the bus. Four of us, Indy in her sunglasses, Zazie with shorts on over her bathing suit (in case we stop somewhere to swim), and Luke tightly holding my hand, unsure but game.

* * *

We flag a tiny, merry bus, bursting with passengers. It clinks along the south shore of the island, east through a forest of brilliant life, through canefields, past schoolchildren, labourers, donkeys, grazing cattle. There's a radio bubbling inside, and the passengers talk and laugh and sway. They coo at Zaz and Indy. Yes, they are twins. Yes, so lucky.

Lukie sits on my lap. We all discuss each others' children. We sleep. Passengers squish in and out of the bus each time it stops. They pay the driver when they get where they're going, handing silver in to him through the window. I pay three dollars for our trip.

Savannah-La-Mar is a fair-sized town, with a traffic jam, a deep-sea harbour, and an indoor market the size of Manhattan. Inside, the bright light is softened, diffused through vast opaque skylights in the vented roof. The heat and din are mixed together by slow-turning ceiling fans. Indy and Zaz experiment with fruits. I can't believe the spice counter.

With Luke on my hip, I examine the many coloured peppers, fresh and dried, hot and sweet, heaped in baskets. Rows of whole spices in bowls: mustard seed, sesame, coriander, cumin and anise. Dozens of ground seasonings: mace, nutmeg, allspice, tumeric and cayenne. Fresh herbs are rolled in newspaper cones: mint, thyme, sage, oregano. There's threads of saffron and branches of laurel and sticks of cinnamon and pods of cardamom and ropes of garlic. There's peppercorns and ginger roots and a lot of stuff I don't recognize. I get little bags of practically everything for Ruthie. The girls choose ackee, plantain, star apples, squashes, coconut, mangoes and avocadoes. Very adventurous.

"What's that, Mom?" says Luke, pointing.

"It's a sweet potato, bunny."

"Oh, wey-o, don't wake him up."

"Okay, we'll buy him quietly."

Nearby are meat stalls with goats and chickens hanging from their feet, eyes closed. The kids think this is pretty gross. They're accustomed to plastic wrap. We wander down the aisles.

On the dock between the water and the market wall, fishermen are bartering last night's catch: spiny lobsters (Ruth was right, these are half the cost of those I got in Negril), crabs, sea urchin, mussels by the bushel, and a rainbow of fishes, unimaginable variety. We go outside to look, and there, bobbing on the afterdeck of a substantial sailboat, is the Italian I saw yesterday afternoon in the Negril bar. He sees me, and to my horror, waves me over.

"You're the family staying at Eve's hotel?"

"At Home Sweet Home, yes," I stammer.

"I know Ruthie. She says you are good people. Jeanie, no?" I stand a moment, surprised. "I am Giancarlo Morosso. Would you like to come aboard my boat?" Nice accent, a rich deep voice. Nice boat, the *Santo Stephano*, a thirty-five-foot wooden ketch, brilliant with brasswork. He waves us forward.

"All right MOM!" says Zazie, stepping over the gangplank. "Wow, Mr. Morosso! Your boat is bee-utiful!"

"Thank you, *signorina*. My brother and I have had very good luck with her since we set out last year."

"You're travelling through?" Hey, I can make conversation, no problem. I see that Zazie is already pretty much up the mast. I get Indy and Luke aboard, and they sit with me on a hatchcover.

"We started from Sardinia, spent some time in the

Canary Islands, and we landed here last summer. Little girl!" he calls to Zazie. "You are up very high! Yes, you are coming down. Good. Please, everyone is free to wander around and explore. *Prego*, Jeanie, can I offer your children some juice? And will you have a glass of wine with me?"

Whew. I shouldn't even be doing *this*. Yes, they're thirsty, thank you. Nothing for me, no, please.

He goes below and comes back with juice and Red Stripes. He says I must have something. Zazie is down now, and we all sit in canvas chairs in the shade of an aft canopy.

Giancarlo is so cordial, but he's also severe, agitated and controlled. We're talking, and he stands up to pace. He has a remarkable mane of hair, a lion chest with the black pelt disappearing into his shirt. His heavy shoulders narrow to smooth hips, his white pants are rolled up to his calves, his wide brown feet pad along the deck.

"Your children are charming!" he yells. He uses a piercing expression when he looks at me, intense and angry, though meanwhile his Italian courtesy floats over all. He's posturing, he's striking poses, for chrissake. He's telling me about sailing in the North Atlantic, while waving his arms and flexing his muscles. He fascinates me: there's at least two people in there.

Giancarlo's brother returns from shopping. As compulsive and vain as is one brother, the other is loose and without pretense. Giancarlo gets up to introduce his sibling, announcing his name loudly, warmly, "This is my brother...Mario."

Mario is a reed-shaped boy, graceful, with leaping eyes, a look of ease and mischief. He is wearing his T-shirt tied on his head, Arab-style. He wiggles his eyebrows at Zazie.

"We're going on a picnic tomorrow," he confides, "to a beach near Negril. Would you like to come?"

"Oh, I must check with my husband, to see what he has planned." I smooth the hair on Indy's forehead. "Thank you so much, though. That's very nice of you." I almost affect an English accent. I feel idiotic.

"He must come too, your husband. And Anicea and her boys. It's a very nice beach, shallow water, and there's a reef nearby. Your big girls can snorkel there." Mario makes it sound perfectly normal, five adults, seven kids, some who met three minutes ago, some not at all. "We'll pick you up at Home Sweet Home at nine tomorrow morning."

What the heck, I think. I'm not busy tomorrow.

"Okay! What can we contribute?"

"You catch the fish," says Giancarlo. "We'll make the *zuppa*."

* * *

We bump home on the bus and drag all our groceries into the kitchen. Ruthie eyes the pile with reserve. It's mid-afternoon, and there is no Frank to be seen.

"Ya west yer money on des avocadoes: dey hard."

I'm really surprised to hear this. Do you have to buy them ripe in Jamaica? "Maybe we'll just leave them for a while, Ruthie, see what happens," I say, placing them in a basket on the counter. As I shove things into the tiny fridge, I describe everything we saw at the market, gush about the spice stalls, rave about the colours, the fish, the fruit. And then there's the Morosso brothers' picnic.

"What do you make of these guys, Ruth? Is this a good idea?"

"Dose boys not dangerous. Different, yeah, dat for sure."

I'm left to wonder different how. Compared to each other? Compared to other tropical boat bums? Other Italians? Hard to pick. Ruth is on her way out.

"They've invited you and Anicea and her kids along," I call after her, inventing her inclusion, "if you'd like to come. How can I reach Anicea to ask her?"

"I see her tonight, I mention it. If she want, she come by."

* * *

Meg and Lyra are sunning on the cliff, playing Scrabble. Zazie has joined them. She's pouring over her letter ledge.

"Oooo, I can make about a million words with these," she enthuses. "Oh, Mom, come and look, this is great." I come around to see what she's got. It's N, D, O, T, X, U, and another N. My daughter is an optimist.

"I'm just looking for a spot to put my word," she says, scanning the board. Her half-sisters are bored or sunstroked. They're wearing hats and sunglasses, gauzy jackets and harem pants, and quarts of Bain de Soleil. Good for them. Meggy is lying on her stomach, propped on her elbows, sweating into a teen magazine.

"Okay, Zazie," she says, "here's a Personality Profile. Are you ready to answer some questions about yourself?"

"Yup," shuffling her Scrabble squares.

"Would you say you were open, cheerful, organized or thoughtful?" Meg studies Zazie over her magazine. Silence.

"All right. Would you say helpful, tense, diplomatic or argumentative?"

"Argumentative," I say immediately.

"I am *not,*" Zazie responds.

"Would you say you were a self-starter? Smart? Purposeful? Or tenacious?"

"Yes!" I offer. Zazie places her word: T U X E D O, using the end of UGLEE. It falls on a double word score. The big girls are appalled.

"Zazie! That is gross! And what's worse! It says here you'd do well running your own business." Meggy snaps closed her magazine.

"Who says you can't believe those things, I dunno," I say.

"I think six is a fine age to enter the world of commerce, Zazie," says Lyra.

"Seen your daddy at all, ladies?" I break in with a nose count.

"No, what? We thought he was with you."

"Well, no. Oh, how was your outing last night?"

"Okay."

"That good?"

Lyra looks up from her book. "Sorry. It was fun, Jeanie. The band was cool, we danced a lot, everybody was dancing."

"And Frank brought you home?"

"Yeah, it was really late," says Meggy. "We got up just a couple of hours ago." She stretches and moves her hair around.

"Did you discuss with your dad, um, what we'll do next time about going out at night?"

"Yeah," Lyra snorts. "I can see why you don't want me to go alone."

"Great. Let's not lose anybody on this vacation."

Lukie comes tearing up, nude as usual. He's full of beans. "AAAAHHHH!" he cries in delight. "Can I pee-ay? I can spey-o!"

"You can't spell," dismisses Zazie.

"And I can move the men around and around!" He slides some letters onto the board.

"Hold it, Luke, leave those letters alone, don't do that."

"Wait, Luke, that's not how this game is played—you have to leave the squares alone." Luke looks up to show he's heard me, but he continues to slide letters. He's got a T and a Q doing battle up in the triple letter score section.

"There he is," says Meggy.

I turn and see Frank stepping down from our treehouse room. He's just waking up, heading for the bathroom. He walks out of sight.

"Oh, good. Kids, I've got something to ask you. We've been invited on a sailboat picnic tomorrow. These people I met today. They offered, I don't get it really, but our Ruthie knows them and she says they're okay. So, would you be interested?"

"Wow, that's cool."

"Yeah, cool, Jeanie."

"Okay. They said that it's a great beach, and you guys could go snorkeling. Need to rent some of that snorkeling stuff up the road, maybe."

"Me too! I love snorkeling!"

"And Zazie too, of course. Yes, and Luke. You should all come with me to get the right-sized flippers."

Frank is vague about where he's been, and he has a hangover. I'm anxious, but I don't push him. I would have gone too, if I'd had a sitter. What's a vacation for? I'm sure he'll tell me about it when he's ready.

Ruthie grills the fish I bought this morning and gives it to us with a mango and chili salsa that is just unbelievable. Bobby and Adele are out for dinner by themselves this evening. Ruth sits with us for a little while before she goes home. She says she's heard from Eve, the hotel owner. Eve's uncle is very sick, and she's going to stay in New York with him. It's funny being alone at the hotel—there's no desk clerk, nobody at all but the dog and us greenhorns. I like it here, and I feel safe, but I just hope nothing odd happens during Ruth's off-hours.

# NINETEEN

Bearing in mind that no one wears a watch, we don't really aim to be ready at nine o'clock. Correctly, Anicea and her sons, Kiehl and Mandra, show up at ten thirty, and the Morosso brothers a half hour later. Frank's up, restored to his usual outwardly focussed self. Ruthie gruffly declines to come along, says she has to watch the hotel. She probably does, and we don't argue with her.

The *Santo Stephano* anchors in the still water off our cliff, and Mario comes over in a rubber dingy to pick us up. We paddle to the sailboat with our gear of sunhats and swimfins and climb aboard by the sea ladder. I introduce Frank to Giancarlo and Mario, and he is energetically welcomed. The little ones put on life jackets, and we hoist sail.

It's hot. There's a great steamy breeze to snap the canvas to life, and we move out smoothly. Out in the open water the wind is stronger. The canvas fills, cracking, and the bow keens through the waves, smashing up dazzling sprays of water. Giancarlo tacks off the wind, and we slow to a more sedate pace. Mario shows the kids how to bait their hooks with squid and everyone trolls. It's brilliant and hot and quiet. Zazie catches the first one, a parrot fish of fair size. Frank helps her wind her reel and unhooks the fish into a pail of seawater. All the kids watch it swimming in there for a while. Anicea's younger boy, Mandra, rebaits his hook with a huge piece of squid. Big game hunter.

We stop at a white beach where palms overhang the sand. Giancarlo drops anchor, and we wade ashore. Mario builds a driftwood fire.

Mario is showing our girls how to get a drink from a coconut. He knows which ones to knock down from the tree. He stands with his brown feet planted wide, whacks off the green coconut top with a machete and gives the first to Indy, who pours the milk down her throat. We all have some of this fantastically refreshing juice, sloshing it on our chests and washing ourselves off in the turquoise sea.

Giancarlo sets a twelve-litre pot of fresh water on the beach fire. He drops a crate of vegetables for the soup near it: carrots, onions, garlic, leeks, fennel, tomatoes. I start cutting. Frank guts the fish that the kids have caught and rinses them. The four smaller children watch him, and push the sand around and explore the treeline, and soon there's a bit of a tag-game going on up there. Meg and Lyra wander off down the beach together to take some photographs. Anicea and Giancarlo sit with me at the vegetable pile, and we peel things and watch the kids.

I'm beginning to feel thirsty when Mario brings me swimfins, mask and snorkel. We walk into the water.

Under the surface is another planet. Sounds are unfamiliar, muffled. There's buoyancy, not gravity, sunlight that's not hot, currents that drag me sideways, fish flashing away into spacy, endless murk. It's a vast blue dimension. I roll in the water: now the mirror of the surface, now the dark depths. There are towns down there, fishy villages.

Mario has a ring in his hand on which he is threading the fish he has caught. The ring is held afloat by a balloon. He dives slowly, slowly down, to the obscure bottom, and then lies there, waiting for a fish. It's a dreamy silent movie. He looks under rocks. He drifts around coral boulders, moving languidly, he can hold his breath forever. His speargun bubbles when it releases. He drifts up with a snapper flipping on his arrow, the diffused light glinting on its scales. Absently, he blows water out of his snorkel tube, hooks the fish through the gills on the ring, bends at the waist and sinks, his legs trailing until he's moving vertically down, just sinks away to resume his hunt. Mario spears four fish. I float on the surface, listening to my pulse and the air passing through my snorkel tube, dreaming.

On the way back to shore, he snatches a crab off a coral table. When we get to the pot on the fire, he drops it into the soup. He winks at me and waggles his head: lucky catch.

* * *

We have cold melon with the soup, Mario's fish grilled on the fire, bread, and rum. Giancarlo eats urchins he has collected. He splits the spiny carapace in two with a scissor tool and scoops the orange tendrils of flesh off the half-shell with his thumbnail. He says the urchin in the Mediterranean is much sweeter, but he has grown to like the Caribbean one.

With their fine sense of Sardinian courtesy, our hosts keep up spirited storytelling through lunch. The brothers bounce their tales back and forth, enriching details and heightening the humour. We are all very comfortable, and after lunch, very lazy. The kids curl up in the shade and close their eyes.

"You look happy, Jeanie." Anicea is lying in the shade next to me, squinting around her elbow.

"I feel happy. I feel new, as if I left myself at home."

Anicea laughs. "New constellations in the night sky, new perspective on the worl', new t'oughts. What is your home like?"

"We have a horse farm in Canada. The land has a stream and some woods. And we each have jobs. Just now, we've been working too hard, and we're wound up. We're beginning to relax slowly since we've been here. It's so different here, Anicea, so much easier to live."

"Not so easy, Jean," she says, without heat. "It a struggle here just to keep de children alive."

"You mean, health care?"

"Yeah."

Okay, I'm picturing low tax base and meagre incomes. I'm seeing a sick baby, and nothing you can do about it. I've seen the school in Negril, too. But I don't say that. "I mean where we live the ground freezes each year, and the sky is covered by cloud for months at a time. Nothing grows, not even the imagination. You must protect yourself from nature, or you'll die. Shelter is vital. So we have two sides to our lives: half the year working to provide for the other half. As a culture, we hoard, we're miserly. It makes us mean.

"Whereas here, we're drunk with the colours and smells. It's passionate, all the senses zooming. Nature gives so much. It's a different meaning to life."

"We see dat, what you said, 'drunk wid nature'. White people wid so much money, an' dey don't work, an' dey don't tink clearly. We see de tourists at der worst.

Westful, t'oughtless. If dat what money do, I don't want it. But de children want de toys. Families get split, Jamaica is split."

"I'm amazed you'll still give us a chance, Anicea."

"You cool, Jeanie. An' I like your kids."

Anicea is sitting now, her dreadlocks held off her neck by a faded wound cloth, a wide-brimmed hat shading her face. She's composed, though intimately present; peaceful, but with her energy right at the surface. I'm in much better contact with her than with my husband. It's the feminine condition.

Frank and I have hardly spoken since he took his girls dancing. I don't want to chase him, but he's not making himself too available. Does this happen to Anicea?

"Do you have help with your boys from their dad?" I ask her.

"He don't need to have babies de way I need dem. Dey part of I becoming Iself. He is Rasta, he seek other ways a growin'."

"Like a monk?"

"Like a monk. He live in de mountains, we see him when we go dere."

"You agreed this together? Separate lives?"

"Separate perspectives. He teaching himself about spiritual refinement. Dey live a harsh life up dere, not for babies. Sometime he ready, and we be together again."

Out in the glare of sea, Frank is snorkeling with Giancarlo. His breathing tube toots along in the waves. Sometimes it disappears, and then it comes back. "Frank and I spend a lot of time apart, but I hadn't thought of it as a bargain, maybe it is."

She's laughing. "Ya don't always sign it, Jeanie."

Mario is wading out to join the snorkelers. He's put

the fire out, the very last of the soup is overturned in the sand. Nothing keeps in the heat.

* * *

Maybe Frank and I do have a bargain. If I really eyeball this thing, I can see that his being home just a few waking hours in a week leaves me to pursue my life completely to my liking. It's sort of a miracle we get along at all.

I have drawn away from him until we barely share our lives. I have nothing in common with his working buddies, the people he spends all his time with, don't even like most of them. I expect to be left on my own with our kids, to a degree, as my mother was alone with me. I keep Frank at a distance, to preserve this familiar order. When he offers to help me, I turn him down. I won't give him a chance to prove he's trustworthy. That's crazy, I see myself doing something that's crazy.

Though mortgaging the farm didn't help. How could Frank not have realized that to me the farm must remain secure, as if it were still Mom's. Dad left us, but we were okay, we had the farm! I can feel myself getting into a spin of anxiety that I know is unreasonable. It's only a mortgage. It can be paid back.

In this life, we attach ourselves to others, even though these attachments can be lost. People die, or by their own will, remove themselves from us. I see that I have recast my friends to replace the missing. Gus I took for my dad, the ideal one, benevolent and nurturing. And I have picked out in Anicea the traits I miss in my mother: her independence, kindness and strength.

What role did I want Frank to play? I suppose...he's

the one I would not lose. But that's impossible: who can endure that burden? I had hoped we would renew our friendship here, but it seems we have different goals.

I cannot dwell on Frank's defection. Collapse occurs to those have time for it. I am insulated from emotional disaster by those who need me to function.

# TWENTY

Zazie can't sleep. The beach is too beautiful, the day too brilliant. She leaps in under our palm fronds, a six-year old cannonball, and lands on my lap. Anicea stirs, checks where her boys are, closes her eyes again.

"Mom, let's go swimming!"

"Soon, my darling."

"I'm hot, Mom. Let's go *now!*" Zazie rests her forehead a second against my neck. "Hot" was her first word. Ten months old, waiting in her highchair, sternly surveying her lunch.

How can I refuse her? She's jiggling on my legs, popping her lips and humming. "Okay, sure, let's go," I say, and we crawl out of the shade and down to the smooth ocean. Zazie has learned to float on her back. She lies there and gazes at the clouds, and at me, without moving her head from the position she has found works for back floating. Girls at sea. We play whale. I'm the enormous mommy, she holds my flipper and glides along beside me. In a while, Indy appears, and she and Zazie play along the shoreline. Luke staggers down the beach with Mandra. Meggy, thank you Meggy, is with them. Frank is not.

Kiehl and Mandra, like many Negril residents, do not swim. The town has a sensational beach which is used exclusively by tourists. The boys sit in the crystal water, their dreadlocks sparkling with spray, enjoying the feel of the foam on their legs. Turquoise water and blinding white sand, soft waving jungle, dazzling chicory sky, and a parrot shrieking somewhere. The boat is bobbing, Giancarlo and Anicea are clattering on board, making ready. Mario is collecting gear, and I come upon him in the water.

"Mario, you were swimming earlier with Frank?"

"He came out of the water with us, Jeanie. After that, I don't know."

Turn to the task. I call to Indy and her sister, "Let's pack up, ladies, it's time we were off." Lyra rouses from her nap. No Frank.

* * *

We don't leave without him. He comes puttering along the beach as we are hustling the kids aboard. He looks blissfully happy and we get underway without discussion. On the trip home, he has a nap. I might kill him.

At the hotel waterfront, Mario helps us unload our gear and lifts the children out of the Zodiac onto the rocky ledge. In the dusk, he waves his T-shirt as he motors back to the Santo Stefano. The ketch is at anchor, cabin lights on, sails furled, mast silhouetted before a fading sky. Tree frogs sing in the gardens, dogs bark down the road. Anicea declines Frank's offer of a taxi home. She holds her little sons by the hand and drifts away into the dark.

There's cold chicken in the fridge and fruits lying around. I had three bowls of Giancarlo's soup, I don't need to eat. The kids have what they want and lie about.

"What a good, endless day," judges Frank. He's pointing his chin up, dangling his arms behind his chairback. Zazie copies his position. Indy is working a loose tooth. Lyra's reading by lamplight. Meggy is mixing fruit juices for a virgin cocktail, and she takes her highball to her room. Luke is lying on his back on a bench.

"I yiked fishing!" he says. "I catched two BIG ones!" The hands held far apart, the age-old fish story.

"You sure did, sweetie. Look out fish! Heeeere's Lukie!" I tickle him, he contracts into a ball. "What was your favourite part, Frank?"

"Oh, I can hardly choose." He rubs his forehead, pleasantly tired. I'm gazing at him as Indy starts to speak. She liked the beach, the palm fort, the swimming. Turning on the bench, Luke adopts his sleeping position.

"And did you see my shells, Mom?" says Indy. "I found some really bee-utiful ones."

"Not as bee-utiful as mine," Zazie shows one from her pocket.

"That one IS mine! I LOST that one!" Indy leaps for Zazie's throat.

"Steady, fellas," I swerve my attention off Frank. "You sound like tired girls to me. Let's get your teeth brushed and hit the hay." They're punchy. They grumble and spit like little cats as I navigate them up to bed. I carry Lukie, deadweight, Fay Wray. Under the mosquito nets, everyone is snoring inside of a minute.

When I get back, Frank is gone. What? What is with that guy?

Ruthie is there though, which is great.

"Hey Ruthie, how is your day going?"

"Not too bad, except we run outta propane for da stove, and I have to change de tanks."

"Oh, heavy. Ruthie, I want to call home, how do I do it?"

I can see I have plummeted in Ruth's esteem. She thought I knew how to use a telephone, for chrissake.

"No, I mean, how will I know how much to pay for the call? Can I use my Bell calling card number? And how long does it take to make a connection? Do I have to reserve a time? Or what."

"We have good service in Negril," she says stiffly. "Just phone! Ask the operator how much. Or reverse de charge."

So I place the call, and sure enough, it goes straight through, collect. Ned answers from the barn. Country music, the familiar acoustic of the stable, makes me very nostalgic. I can smell the straw, imagine the warmth of the horses on a Sunday November evening. I picture Ned leaning on a pitchfork, or braced against bales of straw outside Sunny's boxstall. I want to hear about every single thing.

"Yeah, we're all doing fine, Jeanie. Fair warm today, everybody got outside awhile. Everything's fine."

"Great, and your hip is feeling all right?"

"Yep. You got a call this morning from Joaquin, said he'd like you to call him if you get a chance. He left a number."

"Yeah, please give it to me. I should give you the number of this place too. That's why I'm calling you now..."

"Sure. Got a pencil?"

We exchange numbers and bits of news. I tell him about the sailboat picnic, he tells me about the chickens. I ask about the murder investigation.

"I haven't really heard nuthin' new on that, Jeanie. They're still holding that poor bastard Mason Goddart for the stabbing."

"Joaquin mentioned something about him to me. He said Goddart came to see you in hospital that morning, the Sunday morning when they found Gus."

"Yep, he come to visit, 'cause of my fall, gave me some money he owed me. Said he figured I'd need it if I was gonna be laid up, which was damned straight. Didn't mention Gus, I found out about him later. Mason said he was leaving town, going t' Phoenix, but 'course he didn't get to."

"He came into some money, the weekend Gus was killed."

"Yeah, I wondered about that too. But he wouldn't steal it from Gus and then give it to me, would he."

"I'm more confused than ever."

"Hey, Jeanie, just enjoy yer holiday. How many holidays you had, girl?"

"Yeah, right, not too many, this is indeed number one. Thanks, Ned."

"Maybe don't call Joaquin, even, it don't sound like it's too important."

"That's okay, I don't mind. Thanks, but I want to be kept in the loop. Call me if anything comes up. Call me even if nothing does."

I stand still a minute, thinking. This makes no sense at all. Joaquin told me Goddart was a bum, mean enough to kill Gus for his pocket change. But apparently he's so mean he'd show up at the hospital to pay a debt to an injured rider. So...was Joaquin wrong about him? But I've always trusted Joaquin. He's a good judge of character and a good man.

I dial the number that Ned gave me and get Churchill Downs Racetrack. Tanglefoot answers in the shed row office.

"Hey, Jeanie! How 'bout this mess, eh?"

"What are you talking about, Tangle?"

"Well, I'm talking 'bout Meryl, o' course! He was mugged, din't you hear? Two days ago. Stabbed and robbed right here at the track. Joaquin flew in from Toronto this morning, an' he's down at the hospital now with him."

"Holy shit. But, he's okay?"

"He's alive, yeah. They're saying he'll prob'ly be okay. Things just been going t' hell in a handcart, Jeanie. But Joaquin's down here now."

"Did he see the guy? Did Meryl see who hit him?"

"He says no, it was dark. Right here in our shed row, Jeanie. Gives me the creeps."

"Gives me the creeps too. How's Gabby?"

"He's lost it. I'm doing everything here, since Gabby's fallen apart."

I leave my number for Joaquin and hang up with Tangle's words ringing in my ears. I turn away from the phone, and Lyra is sitting at the table, watching me.

"What's up, Jeanie?"

"I hardly know. But Meryl, one of our assistant trainers, has been attacked. Stabbed, as Gus was. My God."

Lyra puts her arms around me, bless her. We sit down.

"He's not dead, they say he'll recover. It's just... What is going on here? And Gabby, the poor old guy, he's not well equipped for life at the best of times, he's cracked under the stress. Tangle says he just sits all day in the stall with Pete's Prayer—that's a horse he's especially attached to, honey. Gabby's an old horseman with a pet, you could say. I wonder, should I fly up there and see if I can help out?"

"Gee, Jeanie, maybe you should…"

"'Cept I can't very well leave everyone here, especially with your father wandering off half the time."

"What?"

Here's a kid who has probably had her fill of women complaining about Frank. "Sorry, honey. I haven't mentioned this, because it really wasn't a problem until now. Frank's been going out by himself without telling me where. He's just having a good time, it's no big deal. "

"But it's awkward at the moment."

"That's it, exactly." Lyra doesn't miss much. In her single-parent family, she's probably had to fend for herself and her sister more than her share. I don't want to load her up. "Don't worry, sweetie. In fact, forget it. We have only three more days, let's just enjoy them. They can live without me a little longer up north."

"Okay, cool. Because I've seen posters for Marcia Griffiths and her band, playing on the beach Wednesday night? I'd love to catch that."

"Great! We'll do it."

# TWENTY-ONE

The sun's been down for hours, and I'm really sleepy. Joaquin hasn't called, and Frank hasn't shown up. Lyra's yawning.

"Joaquin probably stayed at the hospital till they kicked him out. Those two have a lot to work out. And the day starts early at the track. He's not going to call now. I'm going to bed. You okay, dear?"

"I am so ready to sleep. This is so weird of Dad, though."

"Yes, it is. Next time I see him, I'm gonna pin him down and make him spill the beans."

"Right on, Jean."

"No more Mrs. Nice Guy!"

"Awwright!"

We hug and feel our way along the dark paths to our rooms. The kids are peacefully asleep, and I get in under my net.

* * *

Sometime later, I'm wakened by Frank as he climbs into bed next to me. The moon has moved along in the sky. Frank smells of smoke. I pretend to be asleep.

In a while, Frank's breathing is deep and slow, and I'm fully awake. The day's highlights snap through my head in the way they only do to people alone in the middle of the night.

I am a woman rich in children, and I'm deeply grateful for them. I miss my mother. I wish she'd been their gramma. I miss Gus, my surrogate father. I am hungry for family, with a husband who thrives on distance.

How can he resist us? Has he never seen Zazie play Scrabble? Has he seen Luke singing, arms aloft, through a rain of blossoms in our apple trees? Or Indy patiently sorting through fifteen pairs of boots in our mudroom to find her Wonder Woman Pez dispenser?

And particularly, has he seen me, I wonder.

Or am I missing the point. As Anicea said, you don't always sign your contract. It develops and you live it, you are swept along, you just keep breathing.

Or you are a watchful guide, compass in hand. Why did Frank invite us all on this holiday but then choose to vacation alone? I see myself spilling down a street I have not intended. I was mislead, I thought we'd be here together.

If I say to him, "Frank, what is this?", will the turquoise eyes look back uncomprehending, as his voice says "What more could you want?" Or will he be angry: "*Don't interfere.*" Frank has left me out of his decision, so whatever his feelings are, my question will be an intrusion.

From Lyra's surprised reaction tonight, she had not been aware that her dad was AWOL. The kids don't feel let down. And I know I'm not always thinking straight: maybe I'm being unfair? I can't say I haven't been having a wonderful time. It's wonderful here, but I feel something is deeply wrong.

Who killed Gus? Thorn in my side, inescapably, I keep circling back to this. Dreams from which I awake afraid, but can't really remember, of hazardous rooms I must traverse, and lurking peril, and always, loss. Searching for a solution, sometimes searching for a place to hide. Gus was in his car, as he often remained during conversation. Did he know the killer? Were they chatting?

Was it some sort of random looter in a quiet parking lot? No...it couldn't have been. Security is close on the backstretch, all those expensive horses. There's a twenty-four hour guard at the gate, checking security passes, and a nighttime squad car, the very patrolman that discovered Gus's body.

Someone who lived on the backstretch.

It was the end of our season at Woodbine. Change brought tension to a head. Was Meryl violently resentful about losing his job? But, no, he'd already left town when the murder occurred. And yeah, right, I bet he stabbed himself this week just to throw off suspicion.

The mess there must be back there, missing Gus's steady hand, and both Meryl and Joaquin either hospitalized or traumatized. None of those grooms can handle the show, that's why they're grooms! The staff everywhere must be in uproar. Right now there's nobody at the farm in Toronto except about a dozen broodmares and an accountant, and a bunch of stableboys are running the farm in Louisville. By God, Joaquin needs me! At least to field for him in Toronto. I'll try to reach him first thing.

Why did I think coming to Jamaica was a good idea?

I thrash around in bed, glare out the window, twist up the mosquito net, but finally fall asleep.

* * *

The kids wake me, though they're trying not to. The sun is well up, and I've overslept. My husband stirs beside me, and we look at each other dolefully.

"Don't disappear today, Frank," I mutter. "We gotta talk."

Ruth's coffee is as sweet and rich as cake, and we eat ackee patties with it. Winking sunlight on the gleaming palm fronds, Ruthie bustling with her broom, birdsong and dogs barking. Lyra, up and dressed, has stuck her head outside the gate for a millisecond and returned with fresh orange juice. I get on the phone to talk to Joaquin, but he's over at the racetrack grandstand.

The kids mill around, and in time we decide it's a day for the beach. Meg and Lyra go with the little ones back to our rooms to get books and sunblock. I turn to Frank and fill him in on last night's phone calls.

"So, what do you think? I feel like I should fly right up there and see if I can help out."

Frank's skin has turned brown, and the eyes in this dark face are now a startling blue. He looks wary: he's been wondering what I wanted to say to him. He's holding a little fan of coral in his long, brown fingers.

"Jeanie, you don't work for them any more," he says evenly. "If Joaquin needs help, he's going to have to hire somebody. They'll need someone else in the long run anyway."

"Well, that may be true," I agree. "But in the short run, he's got a helluva lot on his plate. And I think these two stabbings are linked. There's some crazy person assaulting people on the shed row."

"For chrissake," he says, heating up, and flipping the coral onto the table. "You're not a private investigator. It's not up to you to solve this crime."

"Granted, but..."

"You could even be hurt yourself. I think you should stay here."

His choice of words is a trigger. "Yeah, well, I think you should stay here once in a while too, buster," I snap. "What the heck have you been doing anyway, out by yourself all the time?" Damn! I wasn't going to do this.

"I'm not out all the time!" he explodes. "You said you didn't want to come! What choice did I have?"

"What?" Outraged. "So my staying home one night as babysitter means I don't want to be with you? I don't believe my ears."

Ruthie comes back into the hut and stares at us. Frank gives an angry snort and looks away. The kids are reassembling nearby with their hats and beach toys, and we're done our argument for now.

* * *

Down the hill and nearing the beach, Frank and I are walking together amid our children and passersby. We have calmed down.

"Okay, I can see how you'd feel left out," he says. "Last night Mario came by in his jeep while you were putting the kids to bed. He invited me to go with him for a drink, and I thought I'd be back in an hour. He was alone, it was a spur of the moment thing. But I should have talked to you, you're right."

"Thank you. I didn't mean to accuse you, Frank. I know you're having a good time, and of course I want you to have a good time. The news about Meryl upset me. Last night I was thinking I was wrongheaded to be here, you know? It's like, duty calls, I should be helping Joaquin, not flouncing around in the palm fronds."

"You are a very responsible person," Frank says, taking my hand.

I give him a little squeeze, and the crisis is over. Unresolved, but over.

We reach a good looking spot on the beach and deploy our gear. The morning passes, we lie in the sun. We get drinks from a beach bar. Lyra and Meggy distribute the juice to the shorter ones, and they all wander off together. The parents lean for a moment at the bar.

"Frank, this has been on my mind quite a bit while we've been here, and I'd like to bring it up with you now?" Frank nods and sips his beer. "I wonder," I say, "if couples do for each other what as individuals they cannot. By that I mean…like, that you're sociable, which I'm not, but I enjoy your stories about the people you have met, and I can leave the work of socializing to you."

"Yeah, that can be," he shrugs. "Or the nurturing. I love how you pay attention to the kids, or the animals, for that matter. I don't have to worry about them, you've got it covered."

"And I love that you are independent," I continue. "I think I almost *like* it that you're away a lot, because I was alone for so many years. You know me, I need a lot of time by myself."

"My turtle," he winks at me.

"A bit withdrawn sometimes, okay. But I can't be looking after the kids in your place. *Kids need their dads*."

But he skips that bit. "Okay, and for my part, I like how independent *you* are, that you're hands on, you can run the farm by yourself. And I love the farm! I love how we've made it self-sufficient, how we are living practically off the grid, and how you can make a meal out of nothing at all but your own work."

"That's what farming's all about." I bite my tongue and don't say "obviously". "So…if partners choose each other to fill out the parts of themselves that are lacking, and which each of them sees as strengths, then they must reconcile living with their differences."

"Ah-hah, the point."

"Which I want to do. I appreciate how you have made our farm work better, and how your job makes our life there secure. I'm concerned though, that you are getting farther and farther away from us." We are strolling back down to Beach Blanket Central. The breeze blows Frank's hair around, and he puts his sunglasses back on.

I sum up. "Are you skipping my point, Frank? Kids need their dads?"

"Taken, Jeanie." The lenses flash in my direction, and he moves off.

"Okay, good," I say.

It's sort of good. He's silent, alienated, and I've muddied up my chance to say my piece. I haven't come clean. What I really want is that he be nearer to *me*, I'm just scared to say so. I want to catch his swinging hand as we walk, but I don't. I want to ask him what he's thinking, behind his mirror sunglasses, but I don't do that either. Just can't get my neck to stick out that far.

Luke staggers away from the water with something heavy. He's looking down and calling up to us. He's got a big pink and tan conch shell, easily eight inches across the mouth, clean and dazzling. With this miracle, we're all back in paradise.

* * *

We buy some pompano from fishermen who've pulled their skiffs up onto the sand, and as we are returning to Home Sweet Home, we find Giancarlo outside our gate. He has rented a convertible, and he is standing by it. In a very short time a little crowd has gathered around us. Some passersby are now repairing the automatic transmission. There it is, spread out on someone's shirt in the dust beside the front tire. Anicea is chatting with another woman under the trees. Two or three Jamaican guys are chest-deep in the manifold. The kids are playing with a homemade scooter, running up and down the stretch of road in front of the hotel. Presently the car is fixed and running, and most of the people nearby get in it. Giancarlo drives us down into town, and everyone gets out.

"Bye, Winston," calls Giancarlo. "Thanks, Peter."

We buy patties from a pedestrian. These ones are filled with callalou and chilies, a jerk pattie. Fiery, and great with a coke. Sun's hot, and the wind is wonderful. It's gusting up my shirt like a freshman.

Back at the hotel, Mario is hosting a small party. He's baking a ganja cake in our newly refueled oven. His Rasta pal Desmond is over, and Anicea, Giancarlo, and a few I don't know. They're talking about Russian philosophers, comparing Ouspensky to the Rastafari spiritual leader, the emperor Hailie Selassie.

"Gurdjieff, Ouspensky's friend," says Mario, "describes the same effort to control common emotions, promote the purity, the integrity of the human spirit. There are just a few truths in this life..."

"Dis is de ting," Desmond agrees solemnly. "He recognize de different states a consciousness, he a cultivated t'inka. Dey say de normal wakin' life a most men is sleep. He aim to awaken. He cool, Ouspensky."

I'm fixing some peanut butter sandwiches for the non-pattie fans in our group, just hanging around, wallpaper. Frank is leaning in, intent.

"And Desmond," he says, "what are you looking for, man?"

"I would be a master of Iself. I would struggle against de expression a negative emotions. Negativity wests time an' strenth. I want to stop wars, and I can do dis if I know Iself, make an ally of Iself."

So that's what those guys are doing up there in the mountains.

* * *

Ruth appears in the common room with a laundry load, and she shows me where she has taken two phone messages for me. There's one from Joaquin and from a guy named Taylor in Toronto. I hand out sandwiches to Luke and Indy and try the number in Kentucky first. This time nobody answers the phone at Churchill Downs at all.

The Taylor guy turns out to be George Preston Taylor, Gus's probate lawyer. His secretary puts me through to his office. I can hear him fairly well over the philosophy tutorial behind me.

"Yes, Mrs. Spring. Thank you for calling. I'm sorry to disturb your holiday. Your housekeeper, Ned, gave me your phone number."

"That's okay, Mr. Taylor, I'm eager to be kept informed in the midst of all these disturbing events. I'm beginning to think I'm crazy to be here in Jamaica."

"When you decide to return, I would ask that you visit our offices, Mrs. Spring. We have set your file aside for you to examine at your convenience. And of course, there are papers to sign to complete the transactions."

"Okay, sure I will. What transactions?"

"The transfers of ownership. Mr. Hampton's farm here

in Toronto was left to you, and we can advise you on the legal and tax ramifications that you will be facing. A number of his horses are also now yours, in intent at least. We must submit the applications for transfer before the ownership is finalized."

"Wow. Which horses are these?"

"His breeding stock, and some racing horses, Mrs. Spring, including two thoroughbreds he added to his will quite recently. He told me you had a great deal to do with their success, and if anything should happen to him, you should be the beneficiary. There's one called Rotation, and Dancer's Logic... Mrs. Spring?"

"I'm still here. I'm...stunned. I heard about getting the farm, but it didn't seem real. And the horses, why, those are his best horses. Rotation...has already won a quarter million dollars."

"Closer to a half million is on record here, but you'll see all that when you come in."

"Thank you, Mr. Taylor, I'll...call you back."

"Very well, Mrs. Spring. But I have one more thing to tell you, and indeed, this is the reason for my presumption to interrupt your vacation with this call."

"Okay, I'm braced: what is it?"

"There is a time sensitivity to this, a stipulation. Mr. Hampton had perhaps a whimsical nature. He told me that he wanted you to continue your career as a rider of racehorses, he said you had a gift for it."

"Uh-oh."

"Yes, Ma'am. The terms of the will require that you ride in a stakes race within one month of the date of this probate."

"Or else what?"

"You forfeit your inheritance."

# TWENTY-TWO

I don't tell anyone. Frank clearly thinks my behaviour strange. After I've berated him for going off by himself, I do the same, emotionally. Bobby and Adele make a dinner for all of us out of our pompano and their blue crabs, and while the card game is getting started I take the little guys upstairs. I stay there with them, watching the stars come out, and mull over the situation.

I've never ridden in a real race before, let alone a stakes event. My attention has always been on the horse, not the competition. I have no savvy about the technique, the backstretch "jockeying for position." The kingly sport itself has never been my game. Uselessly, I remember that I just barely have the nerve to sit on a horse any more. After an hour, Frank comes up to see what has happened to me.

"I'm going to take in the night air, Jeanie. Want to come for a beer to the bar down the hill?"

"Sure I would. Can Lyra and Meg listen for the kids?"

"They've gone across the road with Bobby and Adele."

"Well, we can't leave these guys alone, Frank."

"Just for an hour, honey, they'll be fine."

This stumps me. No, they won't be fine. There's nobody they can call but the doberman, for crissake. You don't leave six-year-olds alone. He knows that. I think he's saying he wants to go by himself. A bit jolting, after our talk this afternoon.

"Well, no, I'd be wondering if they were okay, and I wouldn't enjoy myself. Go ahead if you want to, though. I'm tired anyway." What am I supposed to say? I'm not his mother.

"Okay, I'm not sleepy. I'll just go for an hour."

"Have one for me," I say, in a textbook example of making the bed and then lying in it.

* * *

Morning, I wake from a rough sleep in the same bleak mood in which I spent most of the night. There's the same gorgeous sunshine pouring down out of a perfect sky upon the sparkling sea, same two happy little daughters yawning in their bed on the other side of the room, same bump where Lukie is still snoring, same undisturbed other side of my double bed. Oh, Frank.

"Where's Dad?" says Zazie, pulling on her bathing suit.

"Down there getting breakfast, I guess. Are you waking up, Yukie?" I ruffle his hair and he stirs. I tie a pareo around my chest and look out the window at the sky while I brush my hair. Luke sits up and stands, pulls the tapes off his overnight diaper and drops it on the floor. He's got his father's complexion, and he's evenly brown from head to foot.

"Grab your hats, kids, we're off for breakfast," I say, plucking up the diaper and heading for the stairs. "Got your sunblock, girls?"

Down in the common room hut. Bobby and Adele are up early. They're leaving today. No Frank.

"Morning, guys," I say. "You look different wearing clothes."

"Feels weird too," admits Bobby. "Back to the office

tomorrow, ugh." They are sharing a coffee out of a single cup, each with a hand on the other's thigh. They bug me.

"Frank sleeping in this morning, Jeanie?" says Adele.

"Yes, I suppose he is." Indy looks at me sharply but says nothing. Ruthie gives her sliced mangoes and oranges, and Indy is diverted. Thank you, Ruthie. Do *you* know where Frank is?

Ruthie puts Cheerios in front of Luke. He is telling an anecdote from nursery school, a demonstration of a telescope.

"You would be surprised to see it," he pipes. "Before stey-oscopes were invited, they used rowed up newspapers, and you would be ebbo to see with that. We have a book about it at schoo-oh."

"Really," Bobby enthuses. "What sort of things could they see?"

"I dunno! But they could see *far*." Could they see your father, I wonder.

The girls drink smoothies and, without a word, Ruthie serves me toast with a few perfect slices of avocado. It's ripened in the three days since our trip to Sav-la-Mar. We exchange a look.

"Thanks, Ruth. A nice breakfast treat."

"Yar welcome, Jeanie."

I walk down to the cliffside hut and peer in at the teens. In their dim, still room, they are unconscious, two soft piles of girl. I return to the kitchen.

"Well, my dears, shall we hit the beach?"

Oh yes, we're all ready to hit the beach. "Ruth, can you please tell the big kids where we are if they wake?" I collect our gear, say goodbye to Bobby and Adele, and we set off out our gate. The road is packed as always.

It's another fabulous day, the sun well up in a brilliant

sky, the onshore breeze full of yelling gulls, the sand burning hot. We spread out our beach blanket on what has become our spot, and the kids dig. In about five minutes, a woman sways up to us with a cooler on her head, selling fresh squeezed orange juice, soursop juice, and cold Red Stripe beer.

"Are dese girls twins?" she asks, smiling at them. "I had tree set a twins," she confides, "but dey all die. You very lucky." She plays with them a bit, like a mom does. "I have six living children," she continues in the lilting accent, "but de twins are so special." The miracle of modern medicine. At home, I'm accustomed to the attention of strangers to our girls, and usually it's in the vein of Ripley's Believe It or Not. But here they are regularly congratulated for having managed to stay alive.

I'm struck by this woman's poise, her matter-of-fact manner, in a life of such ferocity. I buy some of her juice, and she sways off. I think maybe I won't complain about anything for a while.

But I have a couple of problems. The missing husband, the dead boss, the impossibly terrifying stakes race ride to gain the multi-million dollar inheritance.

Frank, well, I certainly brought that on myself. Classically, it would have been nice if he'd noted that I was anxious and had stayed home to keep me company. Or insisted, and found a way to take me with him to get my mind off my troubles. But I can't really get hot about it.

And the stakes race ride, that's like a story out of "Fear Factor". Will she risk her life for several million dollars? Hmm. Still undecided. I don't want to mention this to the family until I know what I'm going to do. It's not up for a vote.

* * *

We're back from the beach late morning, and he still hasn't shown up. An accident? A Jamaican jail? Lost on a bender? Meg and Lyra are up and ready for adventure. Ruthie has a message: *"Meet me for lunch at the Chicken Luscious, F."*

Not dead, goodie. I place a call to Louisville and finally reach Joaquin.

*"Ola, chica, como esta?"*

"Joaquin, lord, it's good to hear your voice. But whenever I talk to you lately, something awful has just happened."

"Right, yes. I am noticing this too, *mira*."

"How's Meryl?"

"He's okay, *muy bien,* he's been released. In fact, he is here this morning. We have been shipping horses again, some of the owners have pulled out. Some of our horses are now running with new stables. And some of our horses have a new owner, I hear, Jeanie."

"You have a delicacy, Joaquin, that I admire."

"Thank you."

"I do have a request, my dear. I have two requests, actually. Will you allow me to help you in some way? May I at least tend Gus's Toronto farm and co-ordinate with the Kentucky stables?"

"I'm sure that will be most helpful, *querida*."

"How is Rotation running?"

"She breezing the mile and working the half mile, back and forth, all week. She running good."

"Okay, I wonder if you would enter her in the Clark Handicap? It's at the end of of the month, right?"

"Yes, ma'am. That is a very few days from now. A mile

and an eighth, is quite far for this filly right now."

"Yeah, so give her some distance tomorrow, and the next day, and then let her rest, okay?"

"All right, yes, she will be fine. So, Jeanie, you are aware that Rotation's owner must be here at Churchill Downs for the horse to run in that stakes race?"

"Yes, sir, I am. I happen to know that Rotation's owner will not only be present, she will be the rider."

* * *

The Luscious is a roadside restaurant, a shack about twelve feet square with window shutters wide open to the hot wind, looking out on a crumbling concrete patio, and completely overhung with purple bougainvillia. The kitchen is outside, behind the building. It's cooler that way, I'm sure. The food is wonderful, the beer is cold. Not having electricity isn't holding back the Luscious one bit. Frank is sitting at one of the patio tables when we arrive.

"Hi kids!" He stands up and hails us gaily. Zazie and Luke run to hug him. He smiles at me and Indy warmly, big white teeth, the straight black hair shining loose down his shoulders. The teens spread themselves over an adjacent table. Frank tells us that last night at the bar he ran into Mario, and they sat together for an hour or two before Mario took him to a house up the hill where a dance party was going on.

"It was quite a small house, about the size of this restaurant, with, oh, fifty people dancing in it. Really hot in there, everyone sweating buckets, and the music *just thumping*, and did we dance? I danced with every person there, I met everyone, it was fantastic."

Zazie wants to hear more about what kind of dancing, how all the people looked. Frank gets up and shows her. The teens are mortified, pretending they don't know us. Lukie is whacking his chair rhythmically with a spoon. The proprietress turns up her radio reggae and brings us some rum, feeling festive. Indy wants to go dancing, right now, yipee!

The proprietress is singing out back, her voice is wonderfully deep and the song is not danceable. She is frying things in a cast iron pan on the wood stove, slices of onion, papaya, chilies and red pepper in coconut oil and lime juice. I find this out as I am looking for the washroom. She indicates a sort of open phonebooth in her backyard, a good place for a really short stay, with a little jug on the ground. I squat and contemplate her cooking. She is spit-roasting whole small fishes. She's got aromatic twigs smoking on the fire, maybe fennel. She pokes the vegetables, turns the fish, sings.

I am resolved. I trust Rotation, she's smart, and she won't let me down. I don't even have to win this race, right? Just ride it. Piece of cake.

And then, I can train my own horses. Maybe Joaquin would like to partner up with me? And Frank and I can use our money to improve the lot of our fellow man. Frank can make movies about energy efficiency, alternate power sources, and human dignity. We can afford to send our children to university. Not at all last on my list is that, if Frank leaves me, I can get my farm out of hock.

All I have to do is not be afraid for about two minutes. I can ride one more time, for chrissake. And it would be great if I could get Frank to look after the kids while I go to Louisville.

I can't forget that in a real race, with a purse of a half million dollars, tension might be sort of high. That the fine old competitive racing spirit might like to eliminate uppity rookies who are in over their heads.

I'm finished with the jug. I button up my pants and head back to the table. Frank is still there, anyway. I'd half-thought he would have wandered off. He's telling the kids tales of his adventures last night, how they went back to Giancarlo's boat with a few of the people they had met at the party, and how they had gone fishing at daybreak. The pink dawn, the soft violet sky with golden clouds, the little seagulls bobbing on the glassy swell.

"They were beautiful, these white birds that looked pink. We must get up early tomorrow kids so you can see them." Frank gestures toward the ocean with a long brown arm. "They sit there, so alert and small, just waking up, looking around. The sunrise was fantastic. The sun was striped with colour, like Jupiter. We slid along in the water, the sky moving, the water moving, and the land breathing in between. Mario caught a stingray accidentally. It's a wonderful fish, like a butterfly. He let it go and it surged off—it was amazing."

"Why did he yet it go, Daddy?"

Frank pulls Luke onto his lap. "Mario says it's cruel to catch these fish. They're no good for eating, they don't hurt anybody...really, it's just sport to take them."

"Did it bite his hook, Dad?" Zazie loved fishing off that boat.

"It didn't, and that was the odd thing, it somehow got one of its wings caught on Mario's hook, is all."

And on and on, about why they call them "sting" rays, and how it could happen that in the whole huge ocean a fish could get snagged on a little hook. And Frank tells us that when they all stopped fishing and came ashore it was still early, and the footprints of the seagulls were everywhere on the beach, and in the night there had been tiny pink shells washed up, a whole beach full of minute shells that looked like the cap you get on your fingertip if you dip it into melted pink wax. The kids declare they didn't see any such shells when we were on the beach this morning, which leads their father to an explanation of tides. And there they go, the usual situation, our children entranced by their dad, and no likelihood at all that I will get a word in. He is happy, joyfully sharing with us his pleasure in being kidnapped by this island.

Will he come back to me, I wonder. Look at him. A child on his lap, another's head under his hand, gazing at me. I'd say his cards are on the table. It's like...there's something wrong with me that I want more from him. That I can't rise above my petty longings and accept. Accept him, I mean, not me.

I love this guy. The one who sings to his kids, invents his life and is enthralled by it. The dancer, the fisherman, the one who held my hand in the delivery room. The one waiting for me to make up my mind.

I wish I were home. This sunshine has been nice, but I've had enough now. I'm tired of keeping the door open to you, Frank, handling things by myself, mythologizing for the kids, setting the limits, peeing in jugs, losing you. I'd like to be sitting in my good old barn. And I'd release you from my accidental hook.

"Ahhh," yawns Frank. "Ladies! Thanks so much for lunch. Now, I've got to have a nap."

"A nap! Dad! It's not sleeptime!" The kids are astonished. *They* don't need naps. Dad's so funny. Lyra is sitting up straight, watching.

"Yup, I'm just pooped, and I've got to go now. I'll see you sweeties later." He's on his feet. Bends over me with an arm across my back. "You would have had fun, Jean," he murmurs, and he's off out the door.

Nuts.

"C'mon, Mom! Dad's going!" Zazie hops at my elbow.

"You can go ahead with him if you like… I gotta pay the bill here. Just a minute, take it easy."

"DAD! Can we come with you?" Upset, yelling up the dusty road, but he's already gone. Lyra is sticking with me, Zazie's torn up with uncertainty.

"Hurry, Mom!" Indy joins her at the door. I'm on my feet, fumbling with my wallet, looking for the proprietress. Here she is, coming to see what all the noise is about. I give her some money, and we burst out of the Luscious.

Was this necessary? You jump up and run out with Mario like this? Would you even notice if *I* left?

Hell, that's not fair. Put this aside.

Burning road. We plod uphill past the tiny hotels, Americans in bikinis, dreadlocked vendors, kids circling on bicycles, mothers with groceries balanced on their heads. Infrequently, a car cleaves the pedestrians to the roadsides. The girls squabble absently among themselves: yes I did, no you didn't. Luke is overheated and cranky. I start a round of Inky Dinky Spider that gets them droning along with me. Presently we are back at our hotel.

But Frank is not. Where I expected to see his prone form asleep on the bed there is just the smooth, blank cover.

I sit down and wipe my face. That's it, I'm done. There'll be no holds barred now.

# TWENTY-THREE

We wander down the road to a supermarket, a palatial building easily twenty feet square, on a time-filling shopping spree. I see three deluxe colouring books, two with push-out paperdolls and lots of beachwear, one with superheros. A true find. The store also carries an interesting line of Jamaican memorabilia, including T-shirts and baseball caps, appropriately green, yellow, black, and featuring the ubiquitous slogan "JAMAICA - NO PROBLEM". I buy two of each for the big girls.

Back at Home Sweet Home we sit on the cliff edge for the rest of the afternoon, puttering. Luke, wearing only his hat, is driving his toy cars around the smooth rocks. Lyra is in the water, snorkeling, looking at fish, and Meggy is stretched out on a lounge chair in the dappled shade with her paperback. Zazie and Indianna are making wind chimes with shells they have collected, dangling them with cotton string from fallen palm boughs. Zazie suspends the chimes, swinging in the soft wind, in our bedroom window frame.

I bring drinks from the common room fridge, and Luke begins to work on his new activity book, cutting out a drawing of a superhero, mastering the technique of scissors. No small feat for a three-year-old. "The trick is thumb up," he observes.

Zazie picks up her storybook, but it doesn't interest her.

"You know how in Roadrunner cartoons," she tells Indy, "they colour a piece of rock darker, the one that's going to fall? This story's like that. You know how it will end."

Huh. I never know how anything will end. How can my own child be so worldly? Looking around, I think "*This* is a vacation", we have finally achieved the proper tempo. Tomorrow's the last full day, and we catch the same planes we arrived on for the return trip on Thursday, leaving early afternoon. We could pack in the morning and get the bus to MoBay before lunch.

Meg comes over to sit beside me on the rocks. "Just a couple more days to endure, eh, Meggy? Have you had fun?"

"Sure, it's been okay, Jeanie."

"You miss your friends at home?"

"I miss Mom, I guess." Meggy leans against me.

"Poor duck. You'll see her soon, though. She'll want to hear about all your adventures." I've not asked how she feels about her life, certainly not that her mom and dad divorced, not even that her dad's footloose here on their vacation, that what she gets is me. Luckily, she likes me. I get my arms and one leg around her and for a while we rock gently. She puts her head back on my collarbone, and I rest my cheek on her hair. "Anything particular you'd like to do on your last day?" I ask.

"Maybe get some bikes? Ride up in the hills a bit, look around?"

"Fantastic idea! We can rent bikes up the road. Your dad would *love* that."

"Okay, cool."

The little guys are colouring, cutting and pasting.

"Luke!" Indy snaps. "If you want something, you have to ask for it! I can't read your mind."

"So!? I can't read at AW!" he hollers back.
"All right! You want help with your scissors?!"
"DUH! Yes!"
"Don't 'duh' me, you little rat!" Swat.
"OW! Mom! Indy hit me!"
"Luke, Indy doesn't want to help someone who's yelling at her. Indy, you have to use your words when you're angry with Luke."
Luke has his scissors poised like a dagger. Here we go. "'Scuse me, Meggy, I gotta get up for this..."

* * *

Frank shows up for dinner, sleepy. He says he stopped in at Desmond's place and slept a few hours there. Piss on him, I don't need to comment.

After we eat, he goes up to our room with the little guys, and they all fall asleep under their nets. Lyra and Meg and I walk up to the bike shack, and then ride the rest of the way up to Rick's Cafe. There's a band, and we sit on the rocky patio and watch the people. Some schoolboys come and sit with us for a while, and my stepdaughters are pleased. The kids drink Ting and I have a couple of Red Stripes, and then we teeter home in the velvet dark, braking on the downhills, girls giggling among singing tree frogs and shooting stars.

When we wake, I lasso Frank on the cliff for a little talk. I've let this go much too long, and all I feel now is inflexible resentment toward him.

"I've decided to go to Kentucky, Frank. I'll go home with you and get everyone settled in, and then I'd like you to stay with the kids, so I can do this. I want to find out about the uproar around Gus's death. It's important to me personally. I want to satisfy myself, get my hands on it. Coming here seemed like a great idea and the kids have had a great time, but I feel abandoned by you. I feel like I've been here alone with them, you don't make any sense to me at all. So do this for me, okay? Take care of the kids, so I can get this monkey off my back. Will you do that for me?"

Looking at him straight: "And after that, decide what you're going to do."

Frank hasn't got much to say to that. He agrees, and I don't even have to mention the money.

* * *

Meg, Lyra and Frank cycle off together late morning, with drinks and sandwiches Ruthie has packed for them. Frank is going to show them "The Interior" and is taking a roadmap. After a morning playing on the rocks, Zaz, Indy, Luke and I decide to go out for lunch to the beach bar. We're all somewhat relieved that the vacation is over, and take special note of everything that happens, to preserve it and take it home with us. The flowers have never before been so fragrant, the townspeople so courageous and tolerant. They say the last day of the vacation is the best one, and for us it is.

That evening when Frank and his girls return, Giancarlo, Mario and Anicea join us for a chicken dinner. Frank starts a woodfire in the firepit and places a grill on it. Ruthie splits the chickens and marinates them with a dry jerk rub. Anicea contributes some bluecrabs she has stuffed, and I make rice and peas and an avocado salad. Mandra, Kyle and Lukie play with sand lizards while Meg, Indy and Zazie dress Barbies.

Mario and Giancarlo help Frank roast the chicken, standing in the sparking firelight, drinking rum punch and hooting. Lyra and Anicea stand with me at the kitchen counter slicing oranges and papaya. This community of travelling friends is greatly comforting to me. I watch the moon drifting in the starry sky, the warm wind lifting the palm branches for my last time, and I file this peace away, against the strain that is to come.

"C'mon, Jeanie!" says Lyra. "The Marcia Griffiths concert!" We all go, swinging off downhill to the beach, in the soft night wind.

# TWENTY-FOUR

Friday afternoon, flying into Kentucky, I feel like Sigourney Weaver descending in the elevator in *Aliens*, strapping on gunware and flamethrowers and composing myself for battle. Gus's killer is there, on the shed row, I know he is. And after I get through with him, I'll ride in a horse race among tough jocks who'll dump me if they can, splatter me on the rail. And if I live through that, the course of my life will change.

Frank was stone-faced this morning about my errand to the lawyer's offices.

"What the hell is this all about, Jeanie?" he fumed. "I'd like to know what bug you have up your butt here."

"I can't explain this right now, Frank. I'm late for my appointment."

"What appointment? You are acting extremely strangely."

"Well, I don't have a monopoly on that, now, do I?" I said, the bug speaking. I had told him nothing about Rotation's transfer of ownership, about the stipulation in the will that had me riding. I hadn't told Frank anything at all, and he was frustrated and angry about it. Naturally, he felt that had I been uncomfortable with his behaviour in Jamaica, I should have spoken up. And now he's resentful that he's trapped in the role of the guilty party.

I was going at it that way because I didn't want to be

talking about money and risk while we were angry. I didn't want to see his face change, as suddenly he might have deemed the risk worthy. It's vulgar to bestow a dollar value on your life. Unbecoming in a husband, anyway.

I'm screwed either way. He'll be insulted that I would think the money would matter to him.

Fuck it, I just don't want to go there. One thing at a time.

* * *

Louisville is much warmer than home. It's still fall here. I rent a car at the airport and feel pretty sporty pulling up at the Hampton Farms barn at Churchill Downs. I can see Meryl standing in the office. He's got his left arm in a sling, and he looks up as I slam the car door.

"Hiya there, Jean," he says, raising his free hand. "Lord, girl, looket all them freckles!"

"Hi, Meryl. Yeah, showing up my English heritage there, eh? How are you doing? I heard about your troubles."

Meryl is about thirty years old, a tall, lean, blond Republican who thinks G.W. Bush is a wonderful man. He knows horses, and he likes a joke, but his political views are pretty scary. "I'll mend fine," he says. "Just been one thing after another here though, ain't it? Soon as we're outta the woods, get Gus's affairs all settled, I'm gone, I swear."

"What's that, Meryl?"

He checks the shed row to see who's listening. "It's not getting jumped here, if that's what you're thinking," he reveals. "I was gonna leave long before this. And I'm not homophobic neither. Gus and me got along just fine. And it's not 'cause Joaquin's Cuban! Don't get me wrong on that neither, Jeanie. Live and let live, that's me all the way."

"For gawdsake, Meryl, what are you talking about?"

"Joaquin an' me just can't get straight with each other, if you'll pardon the pun."

"You don't want to work with him."

"That guy is such a worrywart! He's got that fussy thing, you know? Everything's a conspiracy with him. Somebody's always listening." He checks out the office window again. "Ain't you ever noticed that?"

"Humm, no, Meryl, I guess I haven't. I always thought Joaquin had a pretty good head on his shoulders."

"Well, lucky you, but he's driving me nuts. I told Gus, over and over, don't trust that guy."

"They had quite a history, Meryl. Gus wouldn't know what to do with your point of view, there."

"Yeah, I guess. That last week up in Toronto, I tried to convince him to let Joaquin go, but he just got all cranked up. But I told Gus then that I was leaving."

I reel in. Wait a second: is that it? Someone called his old friend foul? Gus had to reevaluate, decide if he was giving the best service to his owners, considering his bias? Was that what was bothering Gus that week?

We are interrupted by shouting in the barn, and we both come out of the office. There's a small crowd down the shed row, and we walk over to see what's going on. Getting closer, we can hear it's somebody howling, and then I see Joaquin standing with a track security guard and a familiar-looking young man whom I eventually place as Pete's Prayer's owner. They are grouped in front of a box stall that turns out in fact to be Pete's stall, and Gabby is in there with him, doing the howling. Gabby is partly hidden by Pete, who is standing quietly in a green-checked sheet. When I come to a stop in front of the stall, Gabby sees me and comes out sobbing to put his arms around me.

"Jean, good God, you're *finally* here," Gabby gasps into my neck.

I hug him and speak over his shoulder. "Poor Gabby, hello. Hiya fellas, what's the matter here."

"*Ola*, Jeanie. Maybe you remember Mr. Charles Miller?" Indicating the young man.

"Yes, hi Chas, nice to see you again."

Joaquin is using his Ricardo Montalban voice. "Mr. Miller has notified us that he is now retaining Bob Stafford as his trainer and has come today to see his horse relocated to the Stafford barn," Joaquin eyes me meaningfully. "Gabby was under the misapprehension that he was to accompany Pete."

"Ohhh, I see," I say. "But Gabby, we need you here. Pete will have a new groom over there at Stafford."

"But I can't stay here, Jeanie," Gabby leans back to look me in the eye.

"Oh, sure," I say, all empathy. "I know you're best buddies with Pete, but hey, you know racing, eh, Gabby? They come and they go."

"You've been a wonderful groom for Pete," puts in Chas Miller, who is too young to grasp the situation. "But well, ha-ha, business is business."

There's a silence among the horsemen present. Joaquin tries to rescue Chas. "Clearly, there's a special bond here, and it would be good management for the horse to be weaned gradually to the new staff."

"Chas," I say, "I'm sure Gabby could supervise the changeover best by taking Pete over and introducing him to his new groom. Have you got him packed up, Gabby?"

"Yeah, but Jeanie, c'mere, I gotta tell you somethin'—there's more to this than meets the eye."

"Okay, meanwhile, we're all fine here now, right?" Looking at the security guy, who shrugs. He's all fine if we are. "And Chas, you'll have your horse delivered within the quarter hour, all right?"

"Well, sure, I don't have a problem with that, Jeanie."

"Okay, now, Gabby, let's go over here, and you tell me what's on your mind." As everyone departs, we withdraw to the feed room.

"Jea-nie! This is hardly somethin' just on my *mind,*" Gabby hisses, eyes blazing and his grizzled chin firming up. He glances out the door, both ways, to see if we are overheard. "I can't stay here, and I ain't kiddin', Jeanie. I *seen* somethin', and if he finds out he'll kill me too."

# TWENTY-FIVE

All of a sudden, I'm no longer indulging a batty old guy with separation anxiety. Did I hear him right? "Gabby, you're spooking me here, what are you talking about?"

"About *Tangle!*" he rasps. "I was there in the shed row when he jumped Meryl! And I think he's the one kilt poor ol' Gus!"

"You saw Tanglefoot stab Meryl?"

"Last Friday. It was late, oh, ten o'clock or so, 'n I was going to bed. My light's out, when I hear scuffling in the breezeway." Distraught, Gabby's wheezing. "I look, and there's Tanglefoot scrambling out of there, running right past under my window, you can't miss the way he runs, eh? An' there's this dark bundle or something on the ground behind him, 'cept it starts moaning and moving a little bit..."

"Oh, poor Gabby..."

"Never been so scared in all my life! An' I'm thinking, Tangle's gone fer help. 'Cept he doesn't come back! So after a few minutes, I go out, see who's lying there, and it's Meryl, panting and holding his chest and bleeding."

"So you called for help?"

"Yep, an' Phil n' Irene from across the way there, they hear me, and finally security shows up. Meryl's passed out by this time, but he told me later he never knew what hit him... But I seen Tangle! I know he done it!"

"But you didn't tell anybody?"

Gabby's old watery eyes flit around. "I bin too scared!" he blurts. "Tangle's my partner, we're a team, like you said. Ever'body knows that! But now he's all full of hisself, he's all over me about how I ain't working, and he's doing everythin'. Calling me awful names and such. I just can't look him in the eye, y'know? I bin hanging out with Pete. Pete understands what's what. We're fine, just us together." He's gripping his ribs as if to keep his body from flying apart.

"Okay, sweetheart," I say. "Everything's going to be okay. We're going to take Pete over to his new barn, you and I, and then you're moving too, I think. You should stay at Gus's place till this blows over." I take his hand. "Be strong, old buddy. We need you now! We're mighty short-handed, and we need somebody here at Gus's with real horse sense, to show those crazy stable boys how to look after things...or else they're going to screw it all up. Can you do this for me, Gabby? Stay at the farm for a little while till we get this worked out." Look him in the eye.

"I dunno, Jean. Tangle..."

"I'm going to look after Tanglefoot. He won't bother you. Listen: you're the knowhow in this outfit, Gabby. I need your expertise now."

He does relax. Lifts his old chin and takes a breath. "Okay, Jeanie."

* * *

After we move Pete's Prayer over to the Stafford barn, Gabby packs some clothes and puts them in the back of my rented car. While I'm waiting for him, I visit with Rotation, who's as dazzling as ever, her sleek, brilliant copper coat gleaming, her dark eyes full of intelligence and light. She lets me hug her neck.

We never see Tanglefoot at all. I go into the shed row office to find Joaquin. He's got the entry papers for the Clark Handicap in there, and I sign them.

"Your jockey licence still valid, *querida*?" he says quietly.

"On paper, yes. In truth, we both know I've never ridden in a race like this, Joaquin. Just a little anxiety, there."

"You be fine, *mira*. You got the best horse, you won't even see the other riders."

"How many horses we got left here, darling?"

"We lose eleven, we have just eight here now. Four babies at the Kentucky farm, including that Dancer's Logic filly, I bring her down. A dozen broodmares left at the Toronto farm, *mira*. Fandangle we shipped out yesterday, he been sold."

"Really. I'm brokenhearted."

"Yes, right. So just Phil and Irene, Gabby and Tangle left here. How is Ned?"

"He's good, recovering. He'll be coming down in a few weeks. He's going to hold things together at the Toronto farm until he's feeling fit again. I'm taking Gabby with me to Gus's tonight. Keep this to yourself, though, okay my dear? It's just...you don't need him here, and he needs a break."

"Sure. He has been behaving so strangely since I get here. What is the matter with him? What did he tell you?"

I'm hesitating, uncertain about setting this all in motion. But Gabby knows what he saw, and it's certainly worth reporting.

"You seen Tangle around this afternoon?" I ask.

"No, he got nobody entered today, he take some time off."

"Joaquin..." I tell him what Gabby told me about Tangle assaulting Meryl.

"I'm scared to report Tanglefoot," I finish, "right now, right before the race tomorrow. That the police would heckle him and then leave, and he'd try to sabotage me somehow, as revenge. I guess that's stupid. Get over myself, right?"

"It was my experience, in Toronto, that Brock guy pick me up? It was sudden, *cara*. Like a fish on a hook. Tangle won't be around to worry you."

"Okay. There's more, I'm so sorry, dear... Gabby thinks Tangle killed Gus."

"Oh, Jeanie." Joaquin crumples right there before me. Tears come up in his huge eyes, and he puts his hand out to the desk to hold himself up. "Did Gabby say why he thinks this?"

I feel his anguish acutely and feel tears coming up too. "He says he overheard him, Joaquin. Tangle was talking to himself in the stall, months ago, back at Woodbine, digging manure and ranting, resentful, really angry. He was 'getting no appreciation'. 'Should be an assistant trainer'. He felt Gus hired on Meryl instead of seeing how good Tanglefoot was, how well he knew horses. He was fuming mad."

We take a moment together. I put my arms up under Joaquin's arms and hug him. We both calm down.

"Tangle doesn't have all his wheels on the road, that's for sure," he says.

"So we'll call the police now, okay? I'm so sorry, honey."

"*Si, muchacha.*"

"But I'm taking Gabby to the farm. I want him out of the way and protected."

"Right, yes."

"So the police will come and pester *you.*"

"I want that. I am expert at that."

"I'll come back tonight and see how you're doing?"

"We have our plan, Jeanie."

I take a breath. "Joaquin, my darling, one thing more. I was speaking with Meryl earlier; he says he's quitting, that he's not comfortable working with you?"

Joaquin nods just a bit, eyes averted, and I continue. "He says he filled Gus's ear about this, up in Toronto. You knew about it, didn't you. But to me, you said they had 'personal differences'."

When he nods again, I see resignation. "Right, yes. Like I tell you, Gus always did all the work. He never complain, eh? He try to do right by everyone." Joaquin rubs his forehead. "Now we will try to do right by him."

* * *

Gus's farm in Kentucky is old acreage that covers rolling green hills with white fenced pastures, a large weatherized barn, sheds, guest houses, a railed training track, and a stately mansion that is fronted by shade trees, pillars and porch rocking chairs. I drive up to the employee townhouse, and Gabby gets his stuff out of the trunk. We get him installed in one of the apartments, and in the late afternoon, we look over the main barn.

Practically empty with just the four two-year-olds in residence, but it's a gorgeous stable, the interior high-lofted and whitewashed, with huge box stalls lined up along gleaming cedar flooring, big airy windows, and wrought-iron fittings on the stalls. Dancer's Logic spies me over her door and snorts her recognition.

"Lord knows what Geraldine will do with all this," I say to Gabby. "Sell it, I guess. Isn't this pathetic? Four horses in a barn that would hold twenty-five."

"She was never real interested in the business," he agrees. "Gus was just about to build that whole new barn, eh? Buy more broodmares. Such big plans. But that's done with now, I guess... Sure, I can look out fer these babies till Geraldine decides what she'll do."

I look around at Gabby with new eyes. "Gus was sinking more money into this place?"

"Oh, lord yes, a big expansion. Din't he tell you all about that? Huh. He sure liked surprises, eh? How 'bout that. By the way, Jean, I meant to say, you sure got freckly in Jamaica."

Gus was full of surprises. I put this away to think about later.

"Freckles? Oh, Gabby. I had to cover up, the sun's so hot. Like a harem girl, in my gauzy outfits. But I had a great vacation. What a place! Let's go up to the house and see what's for dinner, and I'll tell you all about it.

"I'm riding tomorrow—did I mention this? So I won't see you in the morning. But I want you to check these foals out real good for me, okay?"

* * *

Gabby goes to his room after dinner. With the farm staff alerted to the secrecy of his visit, I go back to the track to find Joaquin.

The backstretch is very quiet. A huge moon is rising

over the grandstand and crickets are twirring in the bushes. Joaquin is in the shed row office.

"Tanglefoot has still not returned, *mira*," he says. "I ask security at the gate to watch out for him to show up, call here when they see him."

"What did the police say?"

"That they want to talk to Gabby before they trouble themselves with Tangle. They say maybe tomorrow they talk with him. They say sure, our suspicions are noted. They not too concerned with a murder Tangle may have committed in another country, nor with an assault where the victim is not pressing a charge."

"Oh."

"Right, yes. Isn't perfect. Do you want me to stay around?"

"No. There's no reason to think Tangle would want to hurt me. We've always gotten along pretty well. He doesn't know we suspect him. It's just another Friday night."

"Get some sleep, Jeanie. You will have a wonderful race tomorrow."

I see Joaquin to his car, then walk over to check Rotation. She's lying down flat in the deep straw in her stall, sound asleep. I don't disturb her but lock myself in the shed row office and lie down on the couch.

My left side is good for a half hour, then I try the right. So that's what the sale of the Swiss hotel was about. Gus was just expanding his business. Geraldine used to visit Europe sometimes and stop by the place to ski, but it wasn't Gus's favourite. He used to joke about how much money it was losing.

No great conspiracy, no blackmail, just the waste of a good man, at the hand of an angry one. His brother Bing's take on that was correct, and my suspicions were wrong.

Speaking of wrong, I wonder if I will have a marriage to go back to? Didn't look really promising this morning. Vengeful me, cutting Frank out of my decisions, using him to cover for me, no consultation, no trust. Guess I taught him a thing or two, eh? Feel better now? I'm ashamed. And what if I am injured tomorrow, or worse? I have been arrogant and small. Frank is my partner. How can we fix this?

What's more, I'm not strong enough for this race. Nursing sick children and vacationing, I've lost muscle tone. Those other jocks won't need to tussle me, I'll probably faint and fly off all on my own. Poor Lukie, another terrible accident.

What am I doing? What money in the world is worth this isolated, bone-headed risk?

* * *

Irene wakes me, clanging water buckets outside the window. It's five o'clock Saturday morning, my day to race, get up and *sme-ell* the coffee. Horses are bright-eyed and swaying in their stalls, ready for breakfast, and the craftwagon is circulating, offering honeybuns, doughnuts, coffee and sandwiches to the early risers.

The phone didn't ring. Is Tanglefoot on the grounds? How could he not be here? He's never late for work. Out late on a hot date? Peculiar timing.

I step outside in the chill clean morning. Splash my face at an outdoor faucet, say hi to Irene, and walk over to Rotation's stall.

Tangle's there, hooking Rotation's water bucket into the corner in her box stall. His face rumpled from sleep, hair askew. Like nothing has ever been wrong in the world, and likely never will.

My heart is thumping in my chest, however. I see lots wrong with the world. I hadn't pictured this.

"Jea-nie! Well, looky who's here. Gonna ride fer us, Jean? Thinka that."

"Yeah! Wow, eh? Can't keep me away. I love it here."

"Don't gimme that, Jeanie. I'm up to speed. Hear you're the new owner of this here filly, among others. Just gotta ride in the stakes race today, eh? An' all yer dreams will come true."

"Tangle! What are you thinking? Tell me about this nice fantasy!" Is he sure of his information? Maybe just a rumour? Can I shake his confidence?

"Stop shittin' me, Jean. I got this right from Meryl, the stupid twerp. Blabbing all over. I know what I'm saying. You stand to win a lotta money today." Tips his head back and hoots. "*Wheee!* A lotta money, and I'm gonna have my share. This here's my horse too. Whole damned outfit should be mine. Damn that Gus."

I stand back. He just wants money. He killed Gus. He stabbed Meryl. He thinks he deserves to get a share of Gus's money!

His words are electrifying for me, conjuring memories that shoot through me now, of Gus, fifteen years ago. I was a kid when he took me in, my mother was dying, I needed the money, and he gave me a job.

Gus tended me benevolently from a distance. He was frustrated with me, accepting of me, and he cared about me. And now, he is giving me this challenge to ride a stakes race. Almost joking, he's made it a game, to soften the blow. But it's money to which I've felt entitled, money I've felt he wanted me to have.

Tanglefoot is not entitled. Gus trusted him too, but wrongly. Gus was a gambler, but Tanglefoot is a murderer.

I am no more deserving than Tangle. Just a farm girl. How did I think this future could be mine? I'm popping, my pulse, eyes, thoughts—like my skull is cracking. Panic, panic.

*I am in the race, Rotation is fast, so fast, she is leading, stretching, ten metres between strides, she is radiant and golden as an angel. Tanglefoot has cut the girth. When it finally gives way, it springs, it retracts wildly and circles around, catches her near foreleg. Rotation's flight is stalled as if a stick had lodged in a propeller, and she goes down, hindquarters arcing overhead, cartwheeling, and I am down, landing on the turf inside the dirt track, the other horses thundering past, and the light fading.*

But this scene playing over in my head, it won't happen. Tanglefoot wouldn't sabotage me. We are a pair; I'm no better than Tangle. Except...I'm afraid. My cowardice is choking me like a villain. And I'm ashamed. Every guilty emotion is ringing in me, I'm unworthy, undeserving, humiliated.

"From that last stakes day at Woodbine," Tangle whines. "I saw you two arguing on the shed row? Gus saying he was gonna cut you out? Remember that? I knew then. I knew we had something going, girl. I knew: I help you out, you'd help me."

And I do remember, the fight we had on that cold morning, Gus's last morning, the argument I regret so much. Tangle walking Rotation cool, listening to our shouts, eyes meeting mine just once, registering and planning, and seeing his chance. Oh, terrible humanity.

I'm appalled, both at Tangle's craziness, and at my own weak despair.

"Damn straight, Tangle," I lie. "Today, we're gonna make a killing."

# TWENTY-SIX

They give girls a room of their own off the jockey's change room. The boys are all in there sparring and taunting each other, and I'm all alone today in my cubicle, putting on Gus's black and red silks for the first and last time, battle colours, girding my loins.

In the paddock, there's a news crew. My story has leaked, the Girl Who Would Be Queen. Human interest, sure. A newswoman with thick foundation makeup is pressing for an interview. But I'm in a desensitized zone. I've got my brassiere on inside the shirt, I made sure of that. Otherwise, who cares. Buckle the crash helmet, wave the whip.

Four thirty in the afternoon, and there's Tanglefoot, standing beside Rotation, having saddled her as he always would. Where are the police? Why has he not been apprehended and carted away? My pulse is thudding in my ears. I have lied to him. Lied to my husband. My children. I am corrupt.

I am approaching them, man and horse, and Tangle has fixed his eyes on mine. We have a deal, goddammit. There is honour among thieves. Rotation stands alertly, tall as noon, red as sunset. No blinkers, no shadowroll, no martingale, no pony, she needs no aids to think about her race. Tangle is glowering, menacing, he turns in slow motion and gives the wide white elastic girth another adjustment around her ribs. I am his judge and betrayer, but I stand small beside him like a conspirator, intimidated and scared. He takes my leg and flies me up into the saddle. He gives me a look that is twisted and bitter. He's in control, he's made himself clear: Get me the money, or I'll kill you. He crosses his arms and steps back. He knows me, knows my fear. And I know him, I know he'd do it.

The bugler blows his beckoning call, and we walk leggy through the breezeway under the grandstand, out onto the wide soft track, left, down past the cheering sports fans to the starting gate, the horses skipping with anticipation. Rotation's attention is on her race. Numb, I'm just a passenger.

We're in post position nine, the outside of the pack. We load last, and the sun is low, the light against us as the bell rings, the gates fly open, the horses crouch and spring out of their confinement to the open, the limitless sky.

Everyone shoulders around for a spot to run in, and we settle for something easy, four back from the leader, and three horses from the rail, for the first time past the stands. The crowd roars, binoculars flashing, the sunlight in my eyes blinds the foreground. The track is fast and we are comfortable for the long run. I'm tucked down, pushing quietly, holding her, she knows what to do.

The boys around me were standoffish in the paddock. I'm the only girl, and from out of town, not a regular rider. They figure to bump me in the backstretch, and that's all she wrote. The two riding beside me are yelling at each other about making a wedge between the front runners, shouting "Get real" and "Outta my way". Rotation is feeling good, waiting for her cue, holding her fourth position and not yet sweating. Pass the quarter turn, she's just warming up. I take her wide and get by the two on the rail. Turning sideways to the sunset, I can finally see where we're going.

On the outside is a big black gelding who, under the whip, is making an early move. Barely past us, he veers in, at the head of the backstretch, cutting us off. Rotation tosses her head, blows him off, swerves around him, sets back down to the task. I love this horse. She is flying now, her lungs are as big as ocean liners, her forelegs flinging forward in the red light, shadows long out before us. She takes a little bump from the horse on the rail, she doesn't care. But it's a setup for a box, we're blocked on three sides and helpless. The riders at each side begin to squeeze in, we have no choice but to drop back. Horse on the rail falters. For one second we have luck, there's a hole between him and the hooves of the horse in front. I push Rotation toward it and she goes, shoving her way past the leader, bullying a space for herself along the rail. At the three-quarter pole, she drops into her Austin-Healey overdrive, and these other guys may as well go home.

Coming around the turn to the stretch, she's the most beautiful thing on legs. Does she touch the ground at all? I don't think so. It is my great privilege to be with her at this moment, all the world ahead of her, the streaming sunlight, the stretch before her empty, the race practically won, the future secure.

But I am exhausted. This is a long race, and just staying aboard is beginning to be an effort. My legs are screaming, I'm gasping for breath. On the right, the black gelding is still with us. The race is too long, Rotation is tiring. She has not been brought along for this distance. She's been training for sprints. It's too far to the wire. I haven't the experience to guide her, to have helped her miss the bumping, conserve her energy. I feel her flagging, and I haven't the strength to pick her up.

She sees the gelding coming out of the corner of her eye, and that's all she needs. Rotation bundles herself and releases a tremendous rush, pulling away from the competitor with each stride. I know how tired she is, and I can't believe she's capable of this drive. How does she find the will to try? I hunch down, my face in the flutter of her little mane, and just hang on.

We go under the wire. I glance back and see the others are far down the field. I lift from the crouch and wobble in the irons, leaning on the lines to draw her in, to hold myself on, panting and seeing spots. Rotation bows her chin to her chest and slows. Gallop, canter, jog. We turn and make our way back to the winner's circle. Shaky, I stroke her slick neck.

"If Gus could see you now, girl," I praise her. "You are amazing."

* * *

Gabby is there in the winner's circle, and I'm shocked to see who he's talking to: Frank and Lyra. I wave at them, and hear their voices rise. Gabby comes to catch Rotation. Press and racing officials are milling, flashbulbs popping. Avelino had a leaping dismount we loved to see, where did he find the strength? I take my feet from the irons and slide to the ground. Frank catches me. Lucky, since my legs don't hold.

"She run good, Jeanie," Gabby winks. "You did all right."

"We were just in time," says Lyra, hugging me. "Dad said we couldn't miss this."

"Hiya, Frank," I turn to him. "You found me."

"Our Adventure Seeker," looking into my face, holding me upright. "Get a load of your mom, kids." The track colour commentator steps over with her microphone and we have a fast video interview: Yes, so lucky. Such a great racehorse. Really? That fast? Wow. Yes, this is my family. Yes, I miss Gus terribly. An incredibly generous man. Yes, the horse did him proud today.

Indianna and Zazie turn away from Rotation as Gabby removes her saddle. Luke takes my hand and gives me a squeeze. Gabby leads the horse away toward the barns. Joaquin is beaming nearby. I make my way through to him.

"Joaquin, where's Tanglefoot?"

"He been apprehended, yes, *mira*. Gabby was interviewed by the police this morning, and his eyewitness report of the stabbing will hold Tangle for now. That Brock fella is putting together a case against him for Gus's murder. He was so excited about his inheritance, it seem Tangle been boasting about his skill with a knife."

"So Brock's come through for us, eh?"

"Maybe he's a little sorry for being such a creep."

Tears come now, grief, and relief, the release from fear. Joaquin puts his arm around my shoulders. "Our Gus is proud of you, *mamita*," he says.

Frank is standing near, I glance up at him, grateful. Luke is holding my hand against his cheek, breathing a little hot spot on my skin. And I am revived, brought firmly back to life. Take a deep breath, and welcome the sight of my family.

# TWENTY-SEVEN

You okay, there, Gabby? Want me to take a shift?"

Circling the shed row with Rotation, the sheet peeled back now, draped on her smooth shoulders, Gabby's been walking her for over an hour. Night has come.

"Hell, no, Jean. We're just fine. See our Ro? See how happy she is?"

"She's pleased with herself, all right." I pat her neck as we walk along. "And how are you, my old friend? Satisfied with the way the mystery has unfolded?"

"Oh. Well. Jean," Gabby looks at me kindly, but reserved, like regarding a young fool. "There's never gonna be any satisfaction, of course. Gus is still dead."

We walk along awhile quietly, passing through the yellow glow of shed lamps along the overhanging roof, bright and dim, bright and dim. In their stalls, the horses are chewing slowly on their hay, settling themselves, getting ready for sleep.

"But the mystery is solved, yeah," Gabby continues eventually. "Gus'd be okay with this. That poor idiot Tanglefoot needs care."

I put my arm around his waist as we walk. "Right, my darling. You're right."

* * *

Later, Frank and I are alone, sitting on a couch together in one of the guest apartments at Hampton Farms. There's a fire in the grate, and outside the crickets chirp on the dark Kentucky pastures. Frank's listening.

"It all happened pretty quickly," I say. "Thank God you had the kids safe with you. Looking back, I could have used your level head, I'd obviously lost mine. I was so afraid Tangle would hurt me. I'd invented eight ways he could do it. Just waiting for one of them to happen."

"Not much I could have done, Jean, aside from badger the police to give you protection, which they didn't see any reason to do. Or maybe I could have camped out overnight in the stall with the horse. We don't have these things happen to us every day. We're not long on problem solving techniques in this area."

"Hey, it's okay, please. I could do without this much excitement." I look at him. "Thanks for bringing Lyra with you, it means a lot to me."

"She insisted on coming. She called us to see how you were doing, and when I told her about the race, that was it."

"And you found out about my little contest...?"

"From Joaquin. I called to see how you were, and he was a bit surprised to hear I was out of the loop."

"Ouch. I'm so sorry, Frank."

"I don't blame you. I was behaving like a jerk in Jamaica. No way you could tell me."

I lean over and hug his neck. "Thank you very much."

"And I know you were trying to give me room to make up my mind about our marriage. For a while, I did think I might let go, repeat what happened with Rosanne. It's so seductive, to skip along from one high point to the next, never to, uh, clean up, as it were."

My turn to listen. I'm all ears.

"I think that's come to the end of its appeal, however," he says. "I can appreciate the space between the peaks now, I mean, the process. We have a lot of interesting process in our life."

"I'll say." But I've got one more thing to ask. "Frank, I have to know this. Did you forge my signature to get the mortgage on my farm?"

"Yes, I did, Jeanie," he admits. "It was a guy thing. The bank manager never questioned ownership of your farm."

"Unbelievable."

"I'll never get out of this, will I?"

"No. I know you intended no harm, but you were colossally wrong, and you will never get out of this."

I'm holding all the cards now, but I feel desperate. Money is an awful thing. There was a terrible accident, and good fortune, and bad judgment, and bewildering behaviour, and a family trying to work together. And now, whatever do we do?

"But, are you okay?" he leans toward me.

"Yeah! I'm very okay. Nothing like a little near-death experience to make you appreciate those near and dear."

"So, otherwise, are we okay?" Frank is standing now, tall and lean, and no stranger to rebuke.

"I think we're okay, Frank. We can keep in touch on that." Squint up at him hopefully.

He gives a little nod, and I take a breath.

"Logic is so much bigger, Mom!" The door bangs as the kids burst into the room.

"You think, Lukie?" The sight of him pumps me up.

"Yeah! She's thicker."

"She's a grown-up horse now, with big muscles, just like Lukie!"

Luke stands proudly flexing, and from across the room, Zazie jumps onto my lap. "Feel MY muscles, Mom. Mine are REALLY big."

"Whoa, Zazie, I might hurt my hand on YOUR muscles. You too, Indy, don't hurt me now, with those things."

"You look better, Jeanie," says Lyra, sitting down with us on the couch.

"Yes ma'am. Everything's better now. Here, let me give you a hug. You are a great kid. Thank you for coming up here."

"No way I'd miss this, are you kidding? Pretty cool, Jean. Mom made Meg stay home, though. She had tests at school. Meggy wants you to call her and tell her all about it."

"Okay, I will. So, what's the plan? What adventures await us now?"

"Joaquin and Ned are both wondering that too," says Frank. "You're their employer now, Jean… And someone else phoned, guy named Mason Goddart. Wasn't he the one they thought stabbed Gus?"

"Yeah, he was charged with his murder."

"Well, charges have been dropped, he's out, he called, he wants to know if you can give him a job."

"Yike, I think Joaquin will have something to say about that. But hold everything! Is anybody else hungry? I'm fainting, here."

"I think there's a party starting downstairs, Mom," says Indy. "Smells like Dad's spaghetti, and there's music."

"There is? What are we doing up here then? Maybe there's DANCING!"

# Author's Note

This is a work of fiction.

The places and events are composites of real places and events, except the Home Sweet Home hotel in Negril, Jamaica, which was a great place to stay in 1975.

My dear husband works in the film industry in Toronto, and I'm grateful to him for his resource information. On his bleakest days, however, he would still be incapable of the blythe self-focus which is Frank's flaw.

My parents are steadfast, loving people, my sister and brother are my closest friends and none are given even a cameo appearance in this story.

My four children supplied my best lines, and I hope they find themselves as adorable here as I did watching them grow up.

I thank Sylvia Fraser for her careful reading of a dorky early draft of this novel: she is generous, patient, helpful and, obviously, gorgeous.

I cannot believe my good luck to have been plucked up by Sylvia McConnell and her ever expanding publishing company. She is supportive, inventive, smart, and kind.

This is a story about loss, and I dedicate it to Casey's memory.

Jesse Frayne was born and raised in Toronto. At age five, she started riding lessons; and at age twelve she owned her first horse. At age fifteen, she started working at Woodbine Racetrack as a hotwalker. One of a handful of female riders in the late sixties, she got her Jockey's Exercise Licence and rode mornings on the racetrack. Afternoons, she trained thoroughbred yearlings.

The births of her four children changed her focus and began the process which led to the writing of *Great Food for Happy Kids* (RendezVous Press, 2001). She had previously entered the writing world in 1987 with scripts for a musical children's show on the CBC. *Just Keep Breathing* is her first work of adult fiction.

Jesse and her family currently reside in Toronto.

Printed in the USA
CPSIA information can be obtained
at www.ICGtesting.com
JSHW012026140824
68134JS00033B/2893